Brendan Connell

Unofficial History of Pi Wei

Brendan Connell was born in Santa Fe, New Mexico, in 1970. His works of fiction include *Unpleasant Tales* (Eibonvale Press, 2013), *The Architect* (PS Publishing, 2012), *Lives of Notorious Cooks* (Chômu Press, 2012), *Miss Homicide Plays the Flute* (Eibonvale Press, 2013), *Jottings from a Far Away Place* (Snuggly Books, 2015), *Cannibals of West Papua* (Zagava, 2015), and *Pleasant Tales* (Eibonvale Press, 2017).

Brendan Connell

Unofficial History of Pi Wei

For Shan Ts'ai

Unofficial History
of Pi Wei

The great secret is to take things
with an impassive mind.
— Ma Hsiang

1.

Reeds bow to rising sun, orange blaze—ducks awaken and hidden gods murmur silent prayers. Long ago the lads tied horns to their heads and pretended to be bulls—prancing this way and that, shaking around, wagging their tails. People used to eat fried sandstone. If there was no wine, they would drink thistle extract. A sword is neither empty nor full. East and west. Eye and eyebrow.

A man on horseback gallops delicately through a village. The billion descendants of a termite gnaw at the temple statue. Confucian Apprentice Rong owes ten strings of cash to Private Secretariat Miao, but can't pay. A priest laments that no one follows the ancient customs. A girl while feeding the poultry wonders if she smells romantic. Old man Hsün searches for a cloud with bones.

There is a retired eunuch who sighs as he watches the peach blossoms fall.

A pig dreams of being a lion.

The secret is to have yellow teeth.

The sage has been drinking osmanthus wine for three hundred years.

Pi Jung was a carrier of night soil. He got it where he could—but always tried to get the best in town. He would go around buying shit from various households and then take it outside the city gates and resell it to farmers or those who needed it for their kitchen gardens for a small profit. He fetched the stuff from the outhouses and chamber pots of the wealthier citizens—from the potties of nobles and merchants, officials and scholars. He would cruise by the military barracks and get the strong smelling stuff—the distillation of meat and wine, rough talk and manly vigor. The poorest citizens, however, never wanted to sell him their shit at a reasonable rate—they seemed to think that it was worth more than it was—if he wouldn't pay what they wanted they'd use it themselves!—but anyhow, he knew shit as a fisherman knew fish or a skilled painter knew paint.

When he wanted wine, he would send his wife, whose name was Yi'an, to fetch it for him, for if he went himself to a restaurant or wine shop, they would say he smelled bad and request him to leave. And so, sadly, he did not have any close friends.

Pi Jung's son, Pi Wei, was no more popular than his father. He would often get beat up by the neighborhood boys.

"Your father carries shit! Ha ha!"

"Dung beetle!"

"Maggot!"

"Little pig!"

He got used to being punched and kicked. He would go home crying, and tell his mother what had happened. Instead of comforting him, however, she would just sigh and shake her head and tell him to go and weed the garden. She wished that she had had a sturdier child.

Pi Jung didn't want his son to turn out like him.

"I'm unskilled and illiterate, so the only thing I can do is go around town taking shit. But if our son learns to read and write his future could be gleaming."

"Let's not waste money on such nonsense," his wife would say. "I'm dressed in rags, haven't had a new stitch of clothing since I don't know when. How about you buy me something nice every now and again?"

But Pi Jung insisted, and sent his son off to a tutor once a week for lessons and, in this way, Pi Wei learned the *Three Character Classic*.

At night he would copy out a few lines in his study book:

> Young . . . name . . . sound . . .
> Apparent . . . father . . . mother . . .
> Light . . . in . . . front . . .
> Opulent . . . when . . . queen . . .

"It's so hard!" he would complain.

"Just keep trying," his father said. "Practice makes perfect!"

This life as light as air. People float aimlessly along. Dog and tiger, both want food. Firefly and moon, both do shine.

Hermits and gods—would you really wish to associate with either?

2.

It was the hour of the horse and Pi Jung had just fetched
a nice load of shit from Judicial Commissioner Tsou's
house—shit of crab dumpling, shit wet with spring wine,
that shit of the rich, that shit so fine
and so maybe
everyone is a Buddha
since this is the one thing
they all let go of
with non-attachment
as they watch the moon
and hold their knees.

   Pi Jung was rushing around a corner at the intersection
of Brotherly Love Road and Newly Civilized Avenue, on
his way to take the shit to Old Lady Ch'in, just outside
of West Gate, who would buy it for a few coins so she
could fertilize her beans, when he collided with a man.
The top of the basket on his back opened and the shit
went everywhere.

   "You bastard, you got shit all over me!"

   Pi Jung was greatly embarrassed. He threw his arms
in the air, kneeled to the ground, hit his head against the
dirt and apologized profusely.

"You think your meager apologies can satisfy me?" the man said in a high-pitched voice. He was dressed in a fancy silk jacket embroidered with a pine cone pattern that was now unpleasantly stained. It was Eunuch Sung, the tax collector. Standing behind him were a few of his henchmen, who looked with horror at the condition of their boss's clothes.

Pi Jung was still apologizing as Eunuch Sung began to beat him.

The sound of bones striking flesh could be heard for several *li*. The eunuch certainly knew well how to use his fists and feet! Pi Jung didn't try to defend himself; he merely got up and tried to back away; but Sung didn't show the least mercy. He chopped at his neck and kicked him in the stomach and ribs; punched him in the face and punched him in the solar plexus and chest.

Blood began to run from Pi Jung's nose and mouth. He fell and the eunuch kicked him some more.

Pi Jung was frowning and clawing at the ground. Eunuch Sung stomped on him a few times as if he were a bug, kicked him in the throat, then laughed and walked off, followed by his lads who were also laughing and congratulating themselves on having such a formidable boss.

People stood staring and pointing at Pi Jung. Someone suggested fetching a doctor.

"Too late . . ."

Presently, Pi Wei came running up to him.

"Father!"

"Wei," Pi Jung said, "it . . . was . . . bad luck . . . to be born my . . ."

But he never finished his sentence.

Pi Wei was stunned. He shook his father, and begged him to speak, to move, to open his eyes, but he could not.

A thin man who was standing near stepped up.

"What's the use of complaining? It was Eunuch Sung who killed your father, but he can do whatever he likes. Your father, on the other hand, was a shit carrier. How can the law possibly be on his side?"

3.

Eunuch Sung sat in his chamber drinking Fen Jiu liquor and reading the *Annotated Rhapsody on the Capital of Yang*. Feeling rather bored, he closed the volume and pushed it away. He poured himself another glass of liquor, threw it back in his throat, and set the cup down.

His eyes wandered over to his shelves. On one were a number of choice volumes—manuals, essays, books of poetry, philosophy, literature, dictionaries, reference books. On another was a boat-shaped cup of carved rhinoceros horn, with an anonymous poem inside that went:

> Herbs grow dense around the stream,
> both sweet and for suicide;
> thick forests and distant peaks,
> in your arms my form I hide.
> The marmots live in the rocks,
> are to this mountain tied;
> listen to frogs and crickets;
> watch the chiffchaffs on clouds ride.

Next to this was a small brush pot of carved bamboo.

There was a bottle-shaped lacquer vase engraved with peony leaves and blossoms.

Then his collection of thumb rings—some in jade, some in horn, some in glass. And a simple wooden one which Emperor Ching-tsung of Min was said to have been wearing when he was assassinated.

There were numerous carved jade knick-knacks, such as a leaping fish with a dragon wrapped around it, a neighing horse, a leaf-shaped cup, a man carrying a naked woman on his back, an elaborately carved belt hook that had once belonged to Ch'en Hung-chin, and then, on one shelf, higher than the rest, was a jar—the jar in which his sexual organs were kept. As his eyes set themselves on this, he was suddenly filled with emotion.

He remembered when he had been a child and had dreamed of having a family, of having his own children—but that was before he had been castrated and brought to the imperial court—denied the right to live normally—filled with spite.

"I'm as meek as an aesthetic choice," he thought, "a human catfish, a tiger boy who looks like a girl in green. I've got blemished memories; seeing headless parodies, portraits of ironies, heaven sustained. I'm just your standard eccentric, living off unborn lust, early Sung poetry, a self-proclaimed hero of idolatry, a cretin with the eyes of a newborn calf, the stumbling actor of low comedy. I'm just one of those girls, your average maniac, a slab of fleshy geometry, a worm boy who looks like a dethroned queen, a decrepit teen."

A tear rolled out of his left eye. He wiped it away and then poured himself another cup of liquor.

4.

Sung had been a difficult lad—always up to pranks and getting in trouble wherever he could. At fifteen *sui*, he already had a reputation for performing gross acts, drinking wine and even engaging in light gambling. His mother hadn't known what to do with him. She had hoped that he would achieve great things, but from the boy's actions, it seemed doubtful that such would be his fate. The way he was going it seemed that he would be no better than a gangster—in jail or wandering around with his nose cut off.

"If I were you," Mrs. Sung's brother said, "I would have him castrated and we can see if we can get him into the Royal Palace. They say that cutting off the penis is the best thing for calming down a lively lad."

"You really think you could get him a job at the Royal Palace if we cut it off?"

"It would be a big benefit to have such a thing on his resume."

"Well, better the penis than the nose!"

blood BLOOD **BLOOD**

It hadn't been fun and all that wetting the bed and his voice became rather high.

He started off in the Royal Bakery, then went to the Night Drum Room.

A cute fellow, he had been in high demand. At first the Master of the Chickens would always summon him, getting him to run all sorts of errands. But one day he was sent to the household of General Ch'ung-chih of the Embroidered Uniform Guard to deliver some birthday wine. The general's appearance was imposing and dissipated, his eyebrows sharp as knives, his mouth like a crumbling mountain, and when he caught sight of the young eunuch, he became immediately interested.

"What's your name?"

"Sung Chü-i, but people call me Bai-bai."

The general laughed. "Your skin's as white as a girl's. Come, pour me a drink of this nice wine you've brought."

Bai-bai couldn't very well refuse, so he did as he had been bidden—and he certainly knew how to pour wine—pulling back his sleeve a bit with one hand while he poured with the other, a slight smile on his face like his lips were a new moon.

The general became quite fond of him and would often summon him to his chambers so he could serve him, chat and sing songs for him. His favorite was one titled "Searching for a Ripe Plum in the Night," the words of which were:

> Sauntering beneath the moon,
> my heart like a child's,
> going itter-at, itter-at
> as I smell the scent
> of ripe plum perfume;
> when finally I grasp
> that soft and mature fruit
> I will stay deep with it
> till it's dew-drenched,
> in the misty morning
> hearing the cock it crow.

"You're quite a lad," he told him. "I'd like to do something for you, so whatever you want, just ask me!"

Sung Chü-i had heard that the general was one of the greatest fighters in Ming and so requested that he teach him a bit of kung fu.

"I don't take on students," the general said.

"I am happy to sing for you, massage your palms, and run as many errands as you like," Sung replied, "but if you could teach me how to fight, that would be great. I am a eunuch and people often don't take me seriously. If I knew how to use my fists, it might make up for what I'm missing."

Ch'ung-chih laughed and told him to come back the next day if he wanted to learn a few things.

5.

The next morning Bai-bai showed up in the courtyard and asked to see the general. The latter came wandering out, stretched and yawned. He went over to the young man and slapped him on the face.

"Hey!" Bai-bai said.

The general slapped him again.

"General," Bai-bai complained, "I asked to learn a little kung fu, not to be slapped!"

The general laughed. "If you don't want to be slapped," he said, "then you have to learn how to leap out of the way."

The general's open hand came flying at Bai-bai's cheek and made contact. The servants, standing at the edge of the courtyard, winced at the sound. They all figured that the eunuch's first lesson would be his last, but they underestimated the lad's persistence.

Bai-bai came to the general's every other morning for quite a while. After he had been slapped about ten thousand times, he finally managed to avoid the general's palm.

"Not bad," the general said, "now I'll teach you how to Straddle the Tiger."

Over the next few months the general taught him the Six Harmonies Eight Methods. He also taught him how to fight with a triple tip spear and how to fight with a short sword—whipping it about like the tail of a river fish.

Furthermore, through the general's influence, Bai-bai was promoted to the Baochaosi—the Royal Toilet Paper Department—where he learned to make the best toilet paper under heaven.

6.

A Taoist walks, staff in hand, through the mountains—
past twisted pines and waterfalls that resemble the tied
sashes of prized courtesans; past giant rocks which have
sat still for one hundred thousand years, lost in meditation, and butterflies, which won't live but a day or two,
and flutter around puddles from last night's rain.

"Give up cowardliness," chants the Taoist, in a deep,
slow, meaningful and mournful voice. "Don't rush. You
can fuck later. Yao's fluid, tiger's paws, dog blood, duck
soles. There was once a butterfly that was very odd. It
had sixteen heads, thirty-two wings, plenty feet, and they
called it a god, though the poor beast could not sing.
Delectable, dimensional, sensational, ineffable. There
was once a big bee that was very strange. It had fourteen
heads, sixty-four stings, plenty yellow, and they called it
a god, though its voice really had no range. Immortals
use amulets, as do heroes. Immortals use amulets, as do
heroes. Immortals use amulets, as do heroes. To ward off
evil ghosts. To ward off evil ghosts. If you sleep in the
mountain and wish to avoid harm then make a sleeping-
in-mountain plaque and hang it up near you. Immortals

use amulets, as do heroes, to ward off evil ghosts. To ward off evil ghosts. Predators, drooling wolves, in the black, they can take your body. Can take your body. Immortals use amulets, as do heroes. Immortals use amulets, as do heroes. Whatever wood is easy to find can be used, though that of fruit trees and pines is best. Paint on the wood a figure with six arms. That will stop dragons; melt tigers; blocks ghosts who swallow swallow swallow."

Mr. Su made a sleeping-in-mountain plaque. After making it, he bowed. Mrs. Teng regularly ate fei-shuang powder and was impervious to both extreme heat and cold. Jen P'in placed a t'ien-shui amulet on a shrine on Mt. Mao, and after that no ghosts would go near it.

A solitary temple amid clearing peaks;
a solitary pilgrim quiescence he seeks.

A solitary statue decorates the hall;
a solitary deity, an old antique.

A solitary pot in which to cook millet;
a solitary gentleman gets no critique.

A solitary cup for solitary wine
a solitary temple in this world so bleak.

A solitary truth humbles all sorts of lies
a solitary pugilist never feels weak.

7.

"Who made this?"

The one who asked the question was Lady Ts'ao, the lady-in-waiting to the Empress Dowager. She held a sheet of toilet paper in her hand. There was a stern expression on her face.

Eunuch Shui, head of the Baochaosi, was as nervous as a five-year-old palace maid with a plate on her head.

"Is . . . is there a problem, ma'am?"

"Her Highness wants to know who made this toilet paper. Was it you?"

"No . . . no . . . it wasn't me," Shui said, looking closely at the sheet. "It looks like some of the paper that new boy, Bai-bai made."

The Empress Dowager was in her chamber leaning on a big pink cushion and drinking fragrant Water Fairy tea, when Bai-bai was led in.

"So you are the one who made that new toilet paper?"

"Your Highness!" Bai-bai cried, casting himself on the floor before her.

"It's . . ."

"Yuurhiggghnesssss . . . !"

"It's . . . so so soft! . . . How did you do that?"

"Your Highness! . . . I—Your humble servant, instead of using normal bamboo, used the leaves of white cat bamboo and . . . I mixed in wool from Shensi, and mandarin orange peels . . . and a little sandalwood from Shantung . . . and a touch of incense-cedar . . . and I treated it with special water."

"Special water?"

"Yes, Your Highness, in this world there are more than one hundred kinds of water—some hard, some soft, some bitter, some sweet. For the paper, I fetched special water from the upper pool of the Second Spring Under Heaven, at the base of Kindhearted Hill, in Wusih—the same water the royal physician uses for making medicine. I did this . . . knowing it would be used by your Majestic Personage."

Tears were coming from Bai-bai's eyes. The Empress Dowager pursed her lips and nodded her head.

"So so so so soft," she said. "And it smells nice too."

8.

Eunuch Sung was in the woods at Mt. Jiuhua, collecting treeswift nests to make paper with. He had heard that the treeswift nests of the mountain had special properties and wanted to use some to make toilet paper with especially for the Empress Dowager. He would make some lovely soft paper by mixing the nests with mountain herbs and precious wood. When it was finished he wanted to, using extracts of Chinese indigo and pomegranate peels, paint each sheet with a different floral design—some with lotus, some chrysanthemum—a few dozen sheets done in cherry blossom and some more in citron, to bring luck and happiness.

He climbed up through the trees, a big sack on his back, plucking the tiny nests from the tree branches. He dumped out the tiny egg from this one, the little squeaking chickling from that one, and stuffed the nests in his sack.

"Hey, what are you doing? Don't you know that this is a sacred mountain and shouldn't be disturbed by scavengers? You're killing all the little birds!"

It was a woman. She was dressed in Taoist garb and had a red sash with a peacock and peony pattern around her waist. She might have been around thirty-five or forty *sui*, but it was hard to tell. Her skin was very clear.

Some rather unpleasant words came from Eunuch Sung's mouth. When he was angry, he liked to curse and say foul things.

"It seems that you need to learn some manners," the woman said.

"There's only one little bitch on this mountain who needs to be taught a lesson," the eunuch replied, "and it isn't me."

The eunuch had learned a good deal from General Ch'ung-chih, and thought he might as well stretch his limbs and kick the buttocks of this woman before returning to his nest gathering. He figured she would be easy to beat up since she was small and slim.

He put down his sack and lunged forward, like a bear ready to hug a doe.

She twirled around him and next thing he knew her foot had struck the back of his head. He was on the ground with leaves in his mouth. He got up quite perturbed and attacked her again. His fists rapidly whooshed through the air, but she patted them aside as if they were a disagreeable smell. With large, sweeping kicks, he tried to take her down, but she jumped over them like a little lass skipping rope. She moved her open palms towards him—was like a mother hanging clothes out to dry. When she struck him, it was as if he were being hit with an iron rod. He wondered how her small hands could have so much strength.

Within a quarter-hour he had a bloody nose and his face was covered with bruises.

"You're a eunuch, but you fight like a man. If you keep doing that you will always get your ass kicked!"

"Ma'am—what style are you beating me with?"

"Sleeping Crane Boxing."

He begged for a lesson and so she beat him some more.

"Oh! You really hurt me!"

"That's good."

"Ma'am," he said, "you have to teach me how to fight. Other men have something between their legs that helps them out in life. I, however, have nothing! So I have to rely on acquiring talents. . . ."

"What reason have I to teach a gelded scoundrel like you? I'm here on Mt. Jiuhua cultivating the Way. I only practice kung fu so I don't get harassed. My only interest is to become like the shapeless wind—to produce good cinnabar and make potable gold, thereby restoring my lovely youth. Where did you say you were from again?"

"I'm a eunuch at the Royal Palace in Nanking. I was here gathering swifts' nests and herbs to make special toilet paper for the Empress Dowager."

"Toilet paper . . . Empress . . . Royal Palace? Hmm. Good salt . . ."

"What's that you said?"

"I've heard that at the kitchens of the Royal Palace they only use Turkistan salt."

"It could be."

"I'll tell you what—get me a nice quantity of that Turkistan salt and I'll teach you to fight like a lady."

"Salt? But why do you want Turkistan salt?"

"Because, you stupid fellow—how can I make potable gold without it?"

A few weeks later Eunuch Sung returned to the mountain with a large quantity of Turkistan salt and, in exchange, the woman, whose name was T'ang An-lun, taught him some kung fu.

He indeed did find that her style was more suited to him. Maybe it was because he lacked his sexual organ? He flapped his arms about as if they were wings and raised his knees, strutting around in a most unique manner. He learned to strike and kick with the calm grace of a long-legged bird—to deflect and follow, to speedily attack and softly overthrow.

"You need to be efficient with your movements, like a queen," T'ang An-lun told him. "Soft, like a cat padding through a meadow. Move your hand like this—like you're washing clothes in a brook. Now like this—as if you were fanning rice at lunchtime."

He visited her twice a year for four years, each time bringing her Turkistan salt, each time receiving martial instruction. But then she disappeared. Had she succeeded in making potable gold?

Sung successfully made a great deal of first-rate toilet paper and, having gained the Empress Dowager's favor, was promoted—to the Shangyijian, the Royal Clothing Department—then to the Shangbojian, the Imperial seals Department—and then to the Shishejian, the Outfittings Department.

Later, being seen as a fellow of great ability and trustworthiness, he was sent to Liulin as a tax collector.

9.

Pi Jung's son shed large, pearl-shaped tears.

"Mother," he said, "now that father has passed away, we are left all alone. But don't worry, I will stay by your side and protect you!"

"Yes," she said, "it is a shame your father is dead. Though he really never did much for me, I can't help but feel a little sad. It was never pleasant to have him come home smelling like night soil, but I always served him his soup."

"I'm lucky to have you as my mother," Pi Wei said.

She looked at him in surprise.

"Tomorrow I will search for work," he continued. "I will find a good job and bring you cash."

"Actually," she said, "there's no need for you to worry about me. There's Master Yu next door. He knows your father is dead and invited me to be his concubine. The truth is that I have held him in my heart for a long time and, up until now, have refrained from becoming his only due to the edicts of social custom. But now that I am free to do as I wish, it seems like the best opportunity for me, so that's what I'm going to do."

"Master Yu will be my new father?" Pi Wei asked.

"Well, no, that will never happen. How could Master Yu stand to have the son of your father hanging around? I wouldn't want him to be jealous."

"And me?"

"You'll have to get by on your own. I hate to say it, but, though you came from my womb and drank a lot of milk from my breast, I've never felt great attachment to you. It is almost as if you were not my son at all. I guess I really am a bad woman, but that's how things are. I think your destiny is to be a night soil carrier like your father."

"So you will go to live with him and I will stay here in the cottage alone?"

"I'm afraid you won't be able to stay in the cottage. Mr. Yi, the butcher down the lane, offered to buy it for a reasonable sum, and I said fine. He will be taking over the premises tomorrow, so you're going to have to clear out."

10.

Pi Wei felt miserable. He went off and sat on the side of the street and started to cry. There were ten thousand rooftops in the city, but not one under which he could rest. He got up, wiped his eyes, and moped along—a sad little fellow all on his own.

Some of the neighborhood boys caught sight of him.

"Hey, look, it's that dirty little cunt Pi Wei!"

"Shall we beat him up?"

"Nothing better to do, so why not?"

There were five of six of them and they all came stalking towards Pi Wei.

"Please . . . please . . ." he murmured.

One of them punched him and he fell down. Then he got up and started to run. The boys threw rocks after him, as if he were some unlucky dog.

Pi Wei's mother had given him four cash when she kicked him out of the house. He went to a soup stall and got a bowl of soup and noodles.

"How much?"

"That'll be four cash!"

He was so worried about where his next meal would come from, that he didn't even enjoy the one he had, slurping the noodles down slowly, joylessly.

That night he slept under the Eastern Pearl Bridge. He could hear the people walking above—dragging their feet over the wood. At the hour of the tiger, a drunken man came and peed on him. The sun soon rose, but the world still seemed a dark place to the lad. Passing through the market, he stared at all the fruits and vegetables. Piles of yardlong beans. Cutworm-colored pei tsai. Baby pak choy and dwarf choy sum. Edible luffa and big tiger-ear chrysanthemum. Roseheart radishes and heart-shaped lychees. Beautiful peaches and appetizing longans. Soft and ripe persimmons and piles of sweet melons.

He gazed longingly at all the dainties. Lotus leaf wrapped glutinous rice. Piles of barbecued chicken feet. Stewed pork knuckles. Braised pigs' heads grinned at him and the butcher knives, as they banged against the cutting boards, sounded like drums. The smell of steamed meatballs and barbecued porkbelly. The aroma of black sesame soup. The bun-sellers appeared to him like immortal gods, their lotus seed buns like the stars of the Milky Way.

He looked at the women standing around nibbling on candied dates or fried hawthorn fruit. Peddlers went about selling sweets and nuts. Tea stalls emitting inviting fragrances. Women shopping, vendors weighing, young girls laughing, vendors waiting, feeling fruits, sprinkling salt on meats, smiles flashing, pointing out chickens, selecting fish, pots steaming. A large crowd was gathered around an oil seller who would pour oil into the jars people brought him. Pi Wei wondered why there were so many people there just to watch an oil seller, so went closer to look.

Every time someone would bring a jar to be filled, the oil seller put a coin on top of it, then proceeded to pour oil through the hole in the coin into the jar. Afterwards, he would lift up the coin—always completely dry, without a drop of oil on it.

"See, practice makes perfect!" he would say.

Pi Wei was very hungry. He was tempted to steal a stewed pork knuckle, but didn't dare. He had seen the dozen or so human heads on display at the east end of the market, each in a little cage mounted on a pole, to discourage people from living bad lives, and he didn't wish his own to be in such an ugly position.

"I had better look for work so I can earn a few coins to eat with," he told himself.

Up and down the lanes he went.

"Ma'am, please let me clean your yard."

"Such impertinence! You're not good enough to sweep up my place! Piss off!"

"Sir, please let me help you unload those bags."

"Fuck off, you dirty little thief!"

"Are you hiring today?"

"Who are you?"

"Pi Wei, son of Pi Jung."

"Never heard of him. Now, if you'd just move along."

11.

Hundred Chang Alley. Hour of the horse.

Written in large, gold letters on the sign:

好時光酒

Pi Wei read: "Her . . . she . . . guang . . . jiu . . ." And again: "Good . . . time . . . light . . . liqueur . . ."

Men were sitting at little tables outside drinking wine and eating snacks.

The owner of the shop was named Wang Ying-hsing. Just that morning his wife, Mu-chih, had told him to clean the latrine, but he hadn't got round to doing it yet. It was located in back of the shop, and was an outhouse on a raised platform that one had to go up the steps to reach. You would kneel down and there was a shoot that led to a pigpen below where a pig would gobble up whatever came its way, so nothing was wasted.

Mr. Wang didn't much like to clean the latrine—not because he didn't like to have a clean latrine to use himself, or have one for his clients to use, but because he found it to be an unpleasant duty, so he always tried to avoid it.

"It's not that I mind cleaning the latrine," he told his wife, "it's that I'm just not that good at it!"

"That's because you don't do it enough," she replied. "If you do it more often, you'll get good. After all, practice makes perfect!"

When Pi Wei wandered up that morning and asked if there were any chores he could do, Mr. Wang thought it was a good opportunity to get out of cleaning the latrine himself. It hadn't been cleaned in some time and was especially filthy and he had other things he would have rather done that morning than scrub it.

"Okay," the wine man said, "if you clean the latrine, I'll give you a bowl of millet."

Pi Wei was delighted and immediately set about doing as he had been asked. His father had worked his whole life with human dung, so Pi Wei felt not the slightest ambivalence towards following in his footsteps. He scrubbed away anywhere his hands could reach, thinking if he did a good job maybe the shop owner would give him an extra-large bowl of millet. He used about ten buckets of water and brought in fresh straw for people to wipe themselves with, and straightened out the pornographic literature so it was in a nice, neat stack, then cleaned the steps leading up to the latrine and rubbed down the pig. When he was done, the wine man looked at his work and nodded his head in approval. Pi Wei had really done a great job. Mr. Wang then gave him a large bowl of millet and a half a radish.

"That boy doesn't seem too bright," Mr. Wang told his wife, "but at least he isn't lazy. I think we could get him to do a lot of work for us at very little expense. And we certainly need someone to clean the latrine since, as you know, it's hard for me to find time to do it myself."

"Well," Mu-chih said, "if it won't cost us much it's fine by me. With all the men coming around and drinking wine and always needing to relieve themselves, the latrine get's really filthy, so if we can get this boy to keep it tidy that might be a good idea."

So Pi Wei was given permission to stick around. He would clean the latrine every day, keeping it as neat as a temple or government office, and burn incense sticks in the morning, afternoon and evening, to keep it smelling nice. He was allowed to sleep in a shed in the back, behind the kitchen garden.

The wine man saw that the boy was both strong and eager and would have him do all sorts of menial chores. He scrubbed the pots, washed the cups and chopsticks, weeded the kitchen garden, did the laundry, chopped firewood, milked the pig, swept out the front, delivered bottles of wine, carried love notes for the customers who would sometimes give him a coin for his efforts, and, also, surreptitiously, made a small amount of cash by, now and again, sneaking away a few buckets of night soil from the pig and taking it and selling it outside the city walls, to old women for their kitchen gardens.

One day the boy decided he should sweep out the wine room. It was filled with jars of wine, each one labeled, but because Wang Ying-hsing was not a very tidy fellow, they were in complete disarray. Some were covered in dust, others had their labels facing the wall. Empty wine jars lay on their sides and a ladle lay on the ground. Some broken cups were in a corner, with spider webs attached to them.

Pi Wei swept up and then decided he should put the place in order. He began to rearrange the jars, lining them against one wall like ranks of soldiers, their labels facing out. He took the lid off of one and it smelled sweet. He took the lid off another and it didn't. Just the opposite. The wine smelled really bad!

"This wine must have gone off," Pi Wei said to himself.

He was just beginning to maneuver the jar out the door when Mr. Wang came up.

"Hey, what are you doing with that wine?" the latter shouted.

"It smells like shit, so I was taking it out back to get rid of it. I think it's rotten!"

"You really are a stupid fellow!"

"Yes?"

"Yes! Don't you know that the worst smelling liquor fetches the most money!?! That jar is full of Western Phoenix liquor. Only the best households can afford to drink that!"

12.

Time passed. Autumn turned to winter, and winter was swept away by spring. Pi Wei did his chores. In summer he hung flypaper to catch the flies. In winter he fed coals to the outhouse brazier, so the guests could go about their business in comfort. The Good Time Wine shop, indeed, became known for its quality latrine and it was not uncommon that someone walking through the streets would stop at the wine shop and purchase a drink just so they could use it, rather than the public one, which was quite unspeakable; and it was also true that guests would look forward to the time when they had drunk enough so that duty called and they marched off to the latrine like pilgrims to a revered shrine.

Sometimes Pi Wei would grab some of the literature from the latrine and read it. The pictures he found interesting, and he also learned many new words. There was *Wild Stories from Chengtu, Elegant Vignettes of Spring Learning, Celestial Destinies Remarkably Fulfilled, Marvelous Encounters at the Shaman Mount, Spring Vistas in a Varicolored Valley, A Miscellany for Leisure Hours, Forgotten Encounters of Erotic Love,* and other titles.

Indeed, it could be said that, after a lad read all of that, no one would need to instruct him on what to do on his wedding night.

Pi Wei wondered if he would ever have a woman. But why not? His father had been a night soil carrier and had found himself a wife and they had copulated and produced a son. The idea, this reality, made him sad.

He had not seen his mother since the day she had given him four cash and told him that he had to leave. He wondered if she thought of him every now and again, if she missed him. He hoped so, and his eyes drooled tears.

At night he would lay between a rake and a shovel and think of Eunuch Sung.

"I would like to kill that bastard!" he thought.

He wanted to murder him and eat out his heart.

One day he saw a man going by in a sedan chair, followed by an entourage of five or six toughs. The man had thin lips and no beard and seemed to be staring at a far-away cloud.

"There goes Eunuch Sung," he heard one of the clients remark.

"Eunuch Sung?" he asked.

"The fellow in the sedan chair. He had it cut off. He's the district tax collector. I guess the old saying is true, 'If you want to make money, forget about what's between your legs.'"

Pi Wei almost bit off his own tongue he was so angry. He wanted to run after the eunuch and kill him, but restrained himself. What could a weak fellow like he do against a powerful man like Sung, who had bodyguards and servants?

"One day I will become formidable, and kill that bastard," he said to himself.

Making inquiries, he found out where he lived. A few times he wandered by his residence, which was quite grand and surrounded by a high wall, but didn't dare to so much as let his shadow fall across the gateway.

"I need to get fit," he told himself.

In his spare time he lifted rocks above his head, trying to gain strength. Moving the wine jars also made him strong, and he would go to the wine room and shift them about here and there, lifting some smaller ones above his head, hugging others to his chest; so in this endeavor, as year said goodbye to year, and year bade farewell to year, and a few more years, like beads on a rosary, clicked along, that weak lad became porcelain.

13.

One night, Pi Wei had a strange dream. He was walking through a magnificent palace, every aspect of which was an ornament. Golden eaves overlapped with golden eaves and beams were carved in the shape of dragons, carp and flying monkeys, while thick pillars were painted with intricate phoenix patterns. Down a stairway mounted by carved lions he noticed a number of men proceeding—two of them were carrying something—something wrapped in a white cloth—but Pi Wei was unable to discern what it was. Impelled by a dream curiosity, however, he followed them. They went out the palace gates and then wandered through a dark and frightening wood until they came to a pit. They threw whatever it was they were carrying into the pit, and then proceeded to urinate on top of it. Then they left, laughing and singing:

> My spear sits firm in my hand;
> fit an arrow in your bow.
> The enemy's at our gates,
> they wish our red blood to gush.
> Let the gongs of battle roar;
> let the bastards' fear it grow;

like male ospreys,
our bravery's on display.

On this defense
our lives depend,
so now let us,
our arrows splurge.
With no women to hold us back,
and with minds tenable;
we'll live on
or die this way.

Then they were gone and the only sound was the wind sighing through the trees.

Pi Wei approached the pit. It was filled with feces and snakes. A horrible stench came from it. He rubbed his eyes and then a pretty woman stood before him. She was wearing a cloud dress and had purple hair done up in an extravagant fashion.

Filled with awe, Pi Wei bowed and asked who she was.

"I'm Tzu-ku," she said, "the goddess of the latrine. In the past, the latrine at the wine shop was a real shame. I had a hard time with it as men were always coming in and peeing all over the place and taking no care about hygiene. If a woman ever had to come in to use the latrine, she was always very uncomfortable. Since you came along though, things have been great. I just wanted to come and thank you for keeping the place tidy and sweet smelling with the incense you burn for me, making it so those who access it no longer need to use dried jujubes for nose stoppers."

Pi Wei bowed deeply. He was too shy to say anything.

14.

Neglecting to repair the thatching on his roof, Ma Ch'i felt his toes get damp through the rainy nights of autumn. Every day Li Yong ate vitex mixed with the blood of a green snake traveling south and, eventually, he turned into grass.

1. Pi Wei bows deeply.
2. The old fellow wants yellow wine.
3. Mrs. Wang asks to see the cash.
4. Mrs. Wang gives a cup.
5. The Taoist wants a bowl.

Shin Ch'ung worshipped the goddess Tzu-ku. He rubbed himself down with aloeswood lotion and onycha paste before using the latrine, which he had decorated with red silk curtains and in which he installed a bed and also made sure there was always a wine table present with tasty snacks.

1. Two jars of wine.
2. Two buckets of common people's wine.
3. Unsavory looking characters scheme.
4. Ho Lung asks for the money.
5. Ho Lung gets kicked in the chin.

15.

The half dozen tables set before the wine shop had felt countless cups bang on them and countless elbows lean on them. They stayed calmly meditating despite all this. Merging with the universe. They truly had no eye, no ear, no tongue, no mind.

All sorts of clients came to drink. Husbands whose wives had ceased to furnish them with their love—those husbands who only found solace in drunkenness and the bought embraces of courtesans,—and young men indulging in a few cups, becoming buoyant before going off to meet their sweethearts, some innocent virgins who would offer them perfumed breaths and laughing temptations and slapped them on the wrist when they made any untoward advances. Merchants who had had a good day and others almost bankrupt, spending their last coins on a jar of the best and becoming glassy-eyed when they thought of their children at home who would soon be reduced to eating gruel. Old men sharing a cup as they talked over old times, or others who became besotted grieving over their white hair. Men who cried when they were drunk, feeling sorry for themselves and everyone around them, and others who, after seven or nine cups, became belligerent and wished to fight, insulting everyone, even their closest friends—searching desperately for the taste in the liquor that they were missing from their own lives. Musicians and poets, looking silly with flowers in their hair, sighing together as they filled each other's cups, and speaking in quiet tones about the inadequacy of art. Then the Confucian scholar, who seemed to be having a memorial service in front of his drink; and young men who drank as if in doing so they were achieving a thousand victories and men twice their age who filled cup after cup silently and then went off to assassinate someone according to plan; and fellows who had abandoned all self-restraint and marinated themselves like bits of beef waiting for the stir-fry; and Lord Lu, with his egret feather cap, getting superbly drunk.

On a certain hot and slow day, around the hour of the dog, Pi Wei was wiping down the tables. About half of them were filled with people.

An old man dressed in a bamboo hat, a ragged robe and straw sandals that looked like they were about to fall apart walked up. He was carrying a yoke with two large empty buckets, one hanging from each end. He set the buckets down, took off his hat and sat down himself and told Pi Wei to bring him a jar of yellow wine.

"That fellow doesn't look like he could afford a handful of millet, let alone wine," Mrs. Wang told Pi Wei. "Check and make sure he's got some coins before we serve him anything to drink."

The young man went back to the table and bowed deeply.

"Excuse me, sir," he said.

"The wine."

"Yes, but . . ."

"Wine! Hurry!"

"Sir . . ."

Mrs. Wang, who had been observing this, saw that Pi Wei was a useless fellow. She walked up to the table, pushed the lad aside, and said:

"You have money? We don't give our wine away, you know."

The old man scowled and plopped a handful of cash down on the table.

"I suppose this is what it's like in the city," he said. "I used to buy my booze from Old Lady Liu, on the highway outside the city walls. But she was eaten by a tiger, so here I am."

Mrs. Wang got a jar of yellow wine and set it down in front of him with a cup.

"Hey," the man said, "it will take me all night to drink this jar of wine with this little cup. Bring me something bigger!"

She brought a soup bowl and set it down before him. He filled it up and slurped it off in a few swallows, then refilled it. Mrs. Wang shook her head with disapproval. She, after all, ran a respectable wine shop, not a den for drunkards. The clients at the other tables all stared, some smiling, some making jokes under their breath. An old man whose only friend was a bottle! Ha ha ha!

"An easy mark."

"It's not worth it."

"Nothing better happening."

"Maybe."

"Enough cash to buy a few rounds of dumplings. Free dinner. Why not? Teach the old drunk a lesson."

After the old man had polished off two jars of wine, he rose to his feet.

"Now, if you could just fill these buckets up with the house stuff, I'll be off."

Pi Wei filled the buckets up with common people's wine and the man, after paying, picked up the buckets with his yoke and wandered off, with unsteady steps, the apparatus balanced on his shoulders. The men who had been sitting at the other table—there were three of them—nodded to each other, got to their feet, and followed him with swaggering strides. They were unsavory looking characters—one short and mean, with a little beard and bad teeth; one big and round, with eyes that wandered about lazily in his head, one going north, the other west; the third tall and thin, with sunken cheeks and a face so pale it seemed to have been sprinkled with rice powder.

Pi Wei was familiar with those fellows. They had a reputation for petty crime and he feared they would do something unkind to the old man, so he decided to follow the group. The man made his way down Central Street and then out West Gate. The others, smiling and joking together, followed him at some distance. About a *li* outside the city gates, they caught up to him, with Pi Wei just behind them, ducking and dodging so as not to be seen.

The fellow with the bad teeth, whose name was Ho Lung, after looking about and not seeing anyone on the road ahead or behind, jogged up to the old man.

"Hey, grandpa, why don't you hand over your money."

"And those buckets of wine while you're at it," the tall and thin fellow chimed in. "I think you've had enough already."

The old man ignored them and kept walking.

"Hey, grandpa . . ."

Ho Lung was about to grab his shoulder from behind when the old man bent over and his leg shot up behind him, greeting the younger man's chin. The latter flew backwards, grimacing awfully.

"You bastard!" the big and round fellow with the lazy, wandering eyes said, thinking *we are from the problem earthworm muddy old people they do not respect the young but should have their white hair respect but to feed us still work so they are forced to go to the cup in the same way there are traps for fish there is fish who like worms.*

They all jumped on the old man at once. The old man snatched the teeth from an open mouth. He wiggled like a lizard; his legs whipped about like flags. And then the men were there, laying on both sides of the road, bleeding and nursing their sores. It seemed that they had mistaken a dragon for a snake.

The buckets of wine were still full. Not a drop had spilled.

Pi Wei had seen it all, and was astonished.

"If I could fight like that," he thought, "I could seek revenge for my father!"

The old man was walking away. Pi Wei ran up and threw himself down at the elder's feet.

"Please, Master! Teach me kung fu!"

The old man frowned. "Kung fu? What makes you think a senior citizen like me knows kung fu?"

"But I just saw you beat up those fellows!"

"I didn't beat them up. They just kept hitting their heads against my feet."

The old man wandered off and Pi Wei, after waiting a bit, followed him discretely.

The elder walked along the main road for about three *li*, then turned north onto a smaller road, went past an old temple, a few farmhouses, a monk carrying a pack, a thatched shelter, a thicket of bamboo and prunus, an old post, and soon there were no dwellings—just verdant mountains and steep cliffs.

He turned and walked up a narrow trail—one too narrow and uneven for any sort of cart—a path that wound up and through dense forest, past static masses and gnarled trees interwoven with bands of mist. Pines violently thrust themselves towards the sky. They passed a massive gorge, rose up, and then descended. A mood of pure solitude. A narrow, two-log bridge passed over a lily-flower river. Then, in the distance, in a little dale, there was a dilapidated hut—a thing that looked like it might fall down at any minute—a dwelling so humble that it seemed doubtful if even a mouse or cricket would deign to live there.

But it wasn't too humble for this old chap, who set down his wine buckets in the yard and stretched his limbs.

> A Taoist hut in the mountains;
> a lovely birdsong can't be weighed.

Nature spirits at night they play;
I left the busy streets behind.
My tiny meditation hall;
every day I do as I please.
Dreams have long since ended;
a single moon sits in my cup.

Pi Wei hid behind a boulder and watched the old man, who sat in front of his hut drinking. Soon the sun began to set and darkness fell, and he drank a few more cups, then went inside, but no light was lit.

"I wonder what he's doing," Pi Wei thought.

He tiptoed up to the hut and heard a snoring sound coming from within.

Pi Wei felt worried. Even if he went back to town, the gates would be closed by the time he got there and he wouldn't be able to get back in—it was no short distance, and he wasn't entirely sure about finding his way along the trail in the dark—and he might get eaten by a wild animal as well.

He sighed, then went over to a wood pile, curled up and fell asleep as the moon crept up over the mountains and the cicadas began to trill.

The next morning the old man awoke, splashed some water on his face, urinated by a boulder, and, naked as Liu Ling, made his way down to the woods which lay beyond his residence.

"He must do his morning training in the woods," Pi Wei thought, and followed him at some distance.

The old man walked into a pine forest and approached one tree somewhat larger than the rest and, pushing himself up to it, began to agitate his body. At first Pi Wei was unsure what he was doing, but then it became quite apparent. The old man was having sex with it.

He then returned to his hut, ate some herbs and began to drink wine again, while humming some odd tune and gazing up at the sky. He had drunk half of one of the two buckets of wine the evening before, and he was now working on finishing it off. Pi Wei still stayed hidden. He was worried that the old man would get angry if he showed himself.

> No meat,
> no music,
> just this cheap wine,
> and the sight
> of jade mountains.

The cups seemed to go down easily for that senior and, indeed, if Pi Wei hadn't seen him easily beat up those thugs the day before, he would have thought him to be nothing more than a drunk. Pi Wei, having grown up in the city, had seen a good many brawls, but had never seen anyone fight like this character.

"He's been drinking a lot, so he should be in a good mood," Pi Wei presently thought. "I had better take the opportunity to approach him."

The young man walked up humbly with his shoulders hunched and offered a profound bow.

The old man didn't seem surprised to see him.

16.

Huge white eyebrows, the oozing of retained semen, floated above eyes acute—flickering crows beneath summer clouds. His pupils were square. He didn't seem to be good friends with the comb and had not visited the mirror for one hundred seasons.

"You again?"

"Me."

"Hmm."

"Please, Master, teach me kung fu!"

"I'm just a drunken old man, what do I know?"

"Master!"

"Quit calling me that!"

"Master?"

"Yes!"

"But, then, what's your name . . . Master?"

"When I was young and sucked from my mother's breast, she called me Good as Gold. Later, when I became haughty, my father called me Forever Disrespectful. Now I am old. If people see me on the road they call me a drunkard or mistake me for a beggar. The woodsmen and wandering poets came to discover that my family

name is T'uan, so to them I'm known as Old Man T'uan,
or to some who have seen me up to things . . . Lunatic
T'uan."

"T'uan."

"Yes."

"Master . . . T'uan."

"Do yourself a favor, get out of here."

"If you could first teach me how to box a little, I could
leave happy."

"I have things to do."

"Master!" Pi Wei cried, and jumped towards him with
his arms spread wide.

T'uan's open palm drifted toward Pi Wei, alighted on
his chest in a blast of orgasmic thunder. The young man
flew back about fifteen feet. His eyes rolled around in his
head and he gasped for breath.

"Ma-ma-master . . ." he stuttered.

"Fuck off," the old man said.

Pi Wei started crying. T'uan shook his head and returned to his drinking. Pi Wei went over to the wood
pile, sat on his haunches and sulked.

Thoughts without form.
Not concrete; not radiating.
They don't touch;
are not obvious;
and do not live on or in
or in between.
Because the instinct of the mind
is realistic omnipresent,
it therefore remains unemancipated.

Something came fluttering by Pi Wei. At first he thought it was a butterfly, but then noticed that it was a coin—there were a few coins in fact, fluttering through the air. They went over to the old man who snatched them up and deposited them in his sleeve.

"What's that?" Pi Wei asked.

"Just some loose cash."

The sun slowly slid across the sky. Clouds sat close by. Master T'uan sat leaning against one of the posts of his porch, wine bucket by his side, and dipped his cup. That refreshing taste! And dipped his cup. What a lovely drink! And dipped his cup. . . . Drinking . . . that . . . luminous . . . liquid . . .

He looked in the bucket. There were a few cups left. He polished them off and sighed.

"I drank it too quickly," he said, his eyes looking a little groggy in his head.

"Yes, you did," Pi Wei added, from where he sat.

"One bucket down, one to go."

"At your pace, it won't last long."

"Mm."

"Mmhmm."

"You're the kid from the wine shop . . ."

"Yes."

"I'll give you a little cash. Go back and fetch me some more wine."

"And?"

"What?"

"It's a long way."

"Yes, it's a long way back to town, but I'm still thirsty. And when this second bucket is gone . . ."

"Master, what is it you wish?"

"If you go and fetch me a couple of buckets of wine I might teach you a thing or two."

"A thing or two?"

"A little footwork . . ."

He handed Pi Wei twenty cash and the latter, enthused, bowed deeply. The second bucket of wine was transferred to an old jar Master T'uan had in his residence and Pi Wei, carrying the yoke with the two empty buckets, ran off towards town.

<h1 style="text-align:center">17.</h1>

When Pi Wei got back to the wine shop, Mrs. Wang gave him a hard time. He had disappeared the day before, and she and her husband had had to deal with things all by themselves.

"I'm sorry," he said, "but I got shut out of the city gates and ended up getting lost in a forest, where I fell asleep. But on my way back someone gave me these buckets to fill up with wine, and some cash to pay for it."

"That's all fine, but before you take the wine back to the client, you need to clean up the latrine. People have been pissing all over and it doesn't smell nice! . . . And the dishes need doing too. You'll have to bring them their wine tomorrow."

Pi Wei went and cleaned the lavatory well, washed up the dishes and weeded the garden.

The next morning he asked Mrs. Wang about the wine. She seemed somewhat suspicious—those buckets looked familiar to her—but she filled them up with wine, thinking that at least Pi Wei had made a sale for her— had, after all, brought her cash for it, so why should she complain?

"Come back right away!" she cried out, as Pi Wei made off with the wine.

Balancing the yoke on his shoulders, he rushed out the city gates and along the highway, then turned and went past the old temple, the farmhouses, a scholarly aesthete out for a stroll, the thatched shelter, the thicket of bamboo and prunus, the old post, spidery trees, the colossal gorge, and over the two-log bridge, and, by the hour of the snake, he was at the dwelling of Master T'uan.

The latter was asleep at his doorstep—curled up in a fetal position. A few flies and a single wasp buzzed around him.

"Master! Master!" Pi Wei cried.

The old man opened one eye, scowled, then sat up, stretched his arms, and scratched himself.

"You . . ."

"I brought some wine, Master."

"Hmm."

Master T'uan dipped his cup in one of the buckets and took a drink.

"So?" Pi Wei asked.

"Idiot, I'll give you a few lessons."

"Master, thank you!"

The old man grunted and then dipped his cup for another drink.

"So glad you're happy!" Pi Wei said.

Master T'uan hit him on the head.

"What was that?" Pi Wei asked.

"First lesson."

Your eyes
carry the moon in them.
Your words
make the world seem real.

The next morning, just as Master T'uan was teaching Pi Wei a thing or two, the cash from the wine purchase came floating in.

"Physical stamina . . ." T'uan murmured. "Practice makes perfect." He sucked down some wine. "Stretch your legs in all sorts of ways; be soft and flexible. Jump around like a frog, waddle like a duck, hop on one leg, open your hips, run around in circles. Now stand like a horse, bundle your hands into fists . . . and stay like that for a few hours."

This beautiful life,
it ran up to me.
I feel just like sun on snow.
No one looks at me;
there's nothing to see.

1. The student jumped around.
2. If you want fish, you need a net.
3. T'uan sent Pei Wei off to get more wine.
4. Mu-chih is rather uptight.

"You've been gone for three days!" Mrs. Wang said.

"The gentleman from before gave me more money for more wine."

"Selling a few measures of wine is all well and good, but I would rather have you here to do your chores. Your absence is not appreciated!"

"But, ma'am, he already gave me the cash to pay for it! If I don't bring him the wine I have to give the money back!"

1. Mu-chih's mother's sister's husband who was older than her father disapproved of his wife's sister's daughter who was younger than his son.
2. The student is practicing his punches.
3. The wine is being drunk.
4. The pig is being fed.

Mrs. Wang did not like Pi Wei's behavior. But when he did reappear, he worked at twice the pace that he normally did—cleaning the latrine like a whirlwind, sweeping up here and there, tending to this and tending to that, so they were not quite ready to fire him—and since he also was only paid in millet and radishes, it would have been tough to find someone to fill his position at the same pay rate.

"That lad's up to something fishy," Mrs. Wang said to her husband.

"He seems to be. But our latrine is still the cleanest in town. A lot of clients come here just for that."

"Right, but . . ."

Tzu-ku. He keeps going back and forth, but never forgets to light incense for me.

Mysterious Lady of the Nine Heavens. He is learning martial skills.

Golden Mother of Nacre Lake. The paths are eating up the straw of his sandals.

Mountain Path. He pitter-pats along me, and this keeps the weeds from growing thick over my scalp.

Ching Ch'ing. Sounds like good news.

Udambara Flower. Master Ching sees everything as yellow leaves.

Golden Mother of Nacre Lake. Master T'uan sees everything as wine.

Tzu-ku. Certainly, otherwise how would that lad learn to fight?

"Something's funny," Mrs. Wang told her husband. "I counted the cash yesterday, but today a few coins are missing."

"A few coins?"

"Twenty cash."

"Maybe you miscounted."

"I don't think so. And the same thing happened the other day as well—as a matter of fact, it's happened three times in as many weeks. I hope you're not sneaking off with some of our money and visiting some stupid sing-song girl."

Mr. Wang sighed. He wished he, like many other men he knew, had the budget to visit a sing-song girl, but his wife never let him have any money and he didn't dare steal any from the till.

"Maybe one of our clients is sneaking in and grabbing some cash when no one is looking?" he suggested.

"You could be right. A few of our customers are not the types of fellows I would trust. They're addicted to drinking and sex and have no morals."

"How much cash was missing the last time?"

"Twenty as well."

"And before that?"

"The same."

"A thief who only steals twenty cash!"

"Twenty cash . . ."

"Twenty cash!"

"Twenty cash . . . twenty cash . . . that's how much Pi Wei brought for wine the other day."

"You don't say?"

"And the time before that, and the time before that too."

"Hmm."

"Yes?"

"Seems suspicious."

She marked all the coins Pi Wei paid her with a tiny dot of red.

> When floating cash
> is marked with a dot of red,
> the one who spends it
> could lose his head.

When Pi Wei next came to purchase wine she examined the coins he handed her. Each one had a tiny red dot on it.

"Ah, you little rat! Looks like you've been stealing my money! You must have some insignificant slut you are getting drunk and fornicating with outside the city gates!"

"No—no—no," Pi Wei stuttered, waving his hand in front of him as if he were polishing a mirror.

1. Mrs. Wang yells at Pi Wei.
2. While she is yelling, one of coins in her hand begins to flutter away and then the others follow.
3. "Ah, you've been paying with trick cash!!!"

"You ungrateful bastard! Every time you buy that wine for your 'client' the money disappears. The last time you paid, I marked the coins—now, sure enough, here you are with them again! You think you can pet the cat while pulling its tail?"

"I think you'd better get the hell out of here," her husband added.

18.

"Master?"

"Mm?"

"No lesson today?"

"No wine."

"No wine?"

"No wine, no lesson."

"But your cash isn't good!"

Master T'uan looked at his disciple with disdain. "Such a simple fellow," he remarked and then turned and went within his hut.

19.

"There are other wine shops," Pi Wei reasoned, "but since I have been caught once, word could soon be out on the street about what I'm up to. And I am spending half my time going back and forth to town, instead of practicing kung fu. And that is delaying my revenge! As the saying goes, 'one winter melon is better than one hundred jujubes.'"

He knew a fellow with a horse and a cart.
    "How much would you rent me your cart for?"
    "The cart alone?"
    "No, with the horse."
    "For an hour or a day? For a day or a month?"
    "Just until tomorrow, at around the hour of the goat."
    "Thirty cash."
    "Why so much?"
    "Why so little!"
    "Ten?"
    "Twenty?"

When the sun set, he lingered around the corner of Hundred Chang Alley and watched as the lamps were lit at the Good Time Wine shop. There weren't too many customers that evening and by the hour of the rat there were none. By the hour of the ox, the lamps were put out, and soon after the place was totally silent.

Pi Wei entered the property—tip-toed to the wine room and lit a lamp. He didn't know much about wine, but he knew which ones were the most expensive—the most prized by connoisseurs. There was the famous burnt wine from South of the Sword, Tribute Liquor from Anhui, and five-grain liquor from I-pin—mellow and luscious, nourishing and soft. All of these were very costly, smelled very bad, and seemed to be most loved by high officials and those with the most money. There was wine from Yan prefecture and wine from Ching-yang—yellow wine from Shao-hsing; Lychee fruit wine from Chekiang and apricot blossom wine, that liquid jewel, from Murmuring Jade Village, and jiugui liquor extracted from the Ch'i-liang Cavern. There was Bamboo Leaf Green liquor from Shan-hsi and the famous Spirit Water from Hsü County; Mulberry-fall wine; Mare Treat wine, made from grapes; chrysanthemum wine, cinnamon wine, mutton wine and cow's milk whisky; the unfiltered wine called Green Ants; and Yellow Rose Essence that is mild and fragrant.

The latter was in a big jar almost as tall as himself—one of those two-*hu* jars that were as solid as a wall. It was so heavy that he had difficulty in moving it. He took it and rolled it out of the wine room and, with great effort, got it onto the cart. As quietly as he could—quietly, quietly, ever so quietly as he was able—he hauled out jar

after jar of wine and loaded them up on the cart—some
giant, some medium, and a number that were not big at
all—but all of the best!

He went and petted the pig and then set off:

1. Cautiously cart moves forward.
2. He waits in an alley by the city gates so that, when
   dawn comes, he is the first one out of town.

The cart was very heavy and the horse had a hard
time dragging it and Pi Wei pulled and pulled the horse
along.

> He's pulling a horse at dawn,
> he's drawing a horse along,
> and their reflections can be seen
> in the water of the brook.
>
> The sun begins to rise;
> the birds begin to sing;
> what happiness there is
> on this summer morning.

In the morning light he passed by various people: a
man with a dead pheasant hanging from a stick, a scholar
followed by a servant carrying his zither, a boy leading a
donkey loaded with charcoal. Their eyes wandered over
the jars of wine and he imagined that, looking at them,
many of them longed for a drink. An old man even asked
if he could sell him a cup, but he said he couldn't as it
was destined for a special client. Around the hour of the
snake, he arrived at the trailhead.

"This cart won't go on the trail," he said to himself, "so how can I get all this wine to Master T'uan?"

Then he reasoned: "Well, if Master T'uan got all this fine wine at once, how fast would he drink it? And once it's gone, my lessons would be over."

He tucked the horse and cart behind a conical rock, tied the horse to the branch of a simplified pine, and searched through the hills and, after about an hour, discovered a good hiding place—a cave. It was almost concealed by foliage. A stand of bamboo was growing near it, the leaves reaching out crispy, a chrysanthemum waving off to one side.

1. It is a lot of trouble, but he hides all the wine in the cave.
2. He covers the mouth of the cave with thorny brush, to make the hiding place complete.
3. "No one will find it here," he thinks. "I'll just come and fetch some whenever Master T'uan gets uptight."
4. He returns the horse and cart.

Horse. The mountains are splendid, and there the grass is tensile but sweet, so why must I live in the town?
Pig. The lad is gone, and now I have no one who cares for me.

When the wine jar was opened, it smelled so bad that Pi Wei almost passed out.

Master T'uan took a whiff.

"Hmmm!" he said.

He dipped a cup into the jar, lifted it to his lips, took a sip and nodded his head in approval.

"Where did you get this?"

"From . . . er . . . Two Wells Village."

"That's not so far."

"Right."

"But . . ."

"???"

". . . the only wine shop there is that of Mr. San-shou. He caught on to my floating cash a long time ago. And his wine is lousy—not like this."

"Oh . . . well . . . there's a new place opened called Greatest Wineshop in the World. The fellow who runs it seems very naïve, so hopefully he won't catch on for a while!"

20.

Master T'uan lived alone, and that was the way he liked it. For many years, his only visitor had been the wind. He seemed as one who existed without purpose, a useless fellow. When he was younger, much younger, back when his hair had been black and his spirit muddy, he had spent his days in books. At the age of nineteen he came in first in the county examinations and then wished for nothing more than to pass the national examinations. And so he had learned by rote the *Great Learning*, had studied the *Doctrine of the Mean* until even his acts of defecation seemed virtuous, could have recited the *Analects* backward or in a dream, and knew *Mencius* better than he knew his own father—a military man, who insisted that his son train a bit with a sword and cudgel, know how to shoot a bow.

"That's all fine, but of all the Six Ministries, the one that attracts me the least is that of War. My greatest desire would be to become Vice Director of the Ministry of Personnel."

"One cannot tell the outcome of an exam ahead of time. Many renowned gentlemen have had to take them several times before passing."

"Oh, don't worry about that. I've been studying hard. I can write a ten thousand word essay in the time it takes a fast horse to run three *li*, imitate the calligraphy of Yen Chen-ch'ing perfectly and write poetry in no way inferior to that of Tu Fu. I'll be a *chuang-yüan*."

But government, corrupt beyond mention, had it so all those who passed the examination did so through bribery, and not skill or knowledge, and so his name did not appear on the list of passing candidates at all, let alone him being *chuang-yüan*.

"Don't worry too much about it. The next examination you'll surely make the list."

People's faith in institutions is not broken easily.

And so the young T'uan set himself to his books with more fury than ever, reading as if his life depended on it. His eyes gobbled down the *Virtuous Discussions of the White Tiger Hall*, he awoke to the *Mao Commentary* and went to bed to the *Commentary of Tso*. *The Inborn-Nature Comes from the Mandate* was scrutinized; *Interactions between Heaven and Mankind* was researched. He hummed *Rhymes of the Central Plain* and recited *Luxuriant Dew of the Annals*. Countless times he dipped into *Comprehensive Meaning of Customs and Habits*. He calculated *The Nine Chapters on the Mathematical Art* and then dived into *Exoteric Traditions of the Han Version of the Songs*. He analyzed the *Classic of Herbal Medicine* and parsed the *Canon of Supreme Mystery*; dissected *Return to the Hidden*, and resolved the *Twenty-four Paragons of Filial Piety*.

But after three years, at the next examination, he again failed.

"Your reading has been too discursive. You should have just concentrated on the *Analects*, the *Book of*

Documents, and the *Great Learning*, and left it at that. As the old saying goes, 'no good soup has more than three ingredients.' But don't worry too much. K'ang Ya, that great scholar, had to take the examination eleven times before he passed."

"Yes, at the age of seventy!"

"Well . . . he got a good government position."

"I'm a nobody!"

"The only two ways to advance oneself in this world are through passing the civil service examination, or through military feats. You haven't done very well at the former, so . . ."

And so he discarded his scholarly robes and put on a suit of armor; joined the army—learned military things—how to lunge and kill with the long sword— how to shake the bamboo spear—how to point the way with a shield—was marched to foreign lands. Fought some battles, killed some men, heard arrows flying past his head, saw families displaced, famine, people trying to dig out of strata of sorrow. Learned Leopard Boxing from a companion. At one point he was promoted to Battalion Commander and given a brocade coat to wear, but six months later, for some trifling incident, he was demoted to a common infantryman.

He was captured by the enemy and imprisoned, and then, when hostilities ceased, released; nothing but a winding road before him.

At a tavern he shared a few drinks with a stranger.

"The country cares more for its pigs than its soldiers," the man said in a low voice, leaning forward like a conspirator. "Fearing exile, the generals don't object to impossible duties. To avoid famine, men enlist, only to find themselves the food of crows, or, destitute after battle, wandering the highways like bandits, snatching rice from peasants and fighting over it like dogs. . . . It's clear by your manners that you are some disgruntled scholar who hoped to find his fortune in war, all the while wishing you were in the Ministry of Revenue, with a brush in hand. But government work is the surest way to diminish talent. Studying the *Great Learning*, the *Purple Book of the Ch'ing-yao Heaven* is ignored. Devoting oneself to the *Analects*, one leaves no time for *Sky's Nine Divisions*. Thinking in terms of high and low, great and small, one prejudices oneself against the Way."

"And so?"

"Man lives from breath to breath, never knowing which will be his last. Even the best horse will die young if it is ridden too hard. When men confine themselves to the cities and towns, chain themselves down with duties and obligations, their spirits wither, while, traversing the mountains and forests, being free from the dichotomy of right and wrong, free from the strains of propriety and toil, they move lightly and joyfully, no longer weighed down by the unnecessary. When one lives according to one's own nature, what need is there to adapt oneself?"

T'uan took the man's words to heart and turned his attention to the Way, shaking the dust of the world from his sandals. Wearing a wanderer's hat, he went from place to place. Having to deal with bandits and tigers, witches and vampires, he requested martial arts teachings from some experts—learned Eight Ultimates Boxing from Mr. Four-Foot Beard; learned Five Animals Calisthenics from

Roseate Hawk Sage; studied Heavenly Plum Style under Professor Flower Festival.

Eager for vast spaces, his feet took him from place to place.

An old man who called himself Wind-Swept Taoist, a hermit with hair that hung to the ground and who dwelt by a waterfall, showed him the way to free himself from anxieties. A ninety-year-old woman who went by the sobriquet of Mistress of Fragrant Grass Cave, instructed him in the Method for Walking Yü's Pace.

He sat in meditation for a year on Mt. Wu-tang, and three on Mt. Qiyun.

At first he studied the *Handbook of the Plain Girl,* then the *Handbook of Master Jung-ch'eng,* and after that the *Handbook of the Dark Girl.* Then an immortal on Mt. Qingcheng, who was known as Bamboo-Cutting Master, gave him the *Mysterious Scripture of Tree Sex Inscribed by the Worthy of the Big Dipper,* together with oral transmission, and the pieces all fit in place.

Seeing that the social climate of the times was unfavorable, he abandoned having to do with men—disdaining riches and honors in favor of wind and dust. When, by chance, he heard a new emperor had ascended the throne, or his country had just been defeated in a great battle, he would just laugh.

Living in obscurity felt great to him. He needed no friend but the wine jar, no one to embrace but trees. And so he spent his days relaxing in the sun, letting insects buzz about him—writing poems on the breeze and painting pictures on the sky.

Verdant peaks above the clouds;
cross your legs, relax your mind.
Hermits and gods live up there;
prayers said to flowing streams.
Some must be shouted loud;
cover ears, hear everything.
Stepping lightly, pluck some herbs;
I sit, away from the crowds.

21.

"The wine house has been raided!"

"Something's missing?"

"All the good wine!"

"The Double-distilled Fen?"

"Yes!"

"The Mt. Elephant Three Flowers?"

"Yes! Yes!"

"It sells for three hundred cash a peck! Who the hell . . . ?"

"It surely is that scoundrel Pi Wei! We treated him so well and he turned into a thief!"

22.

Eat fish in the wild mulberry.

Mysterious cranes stand in the reeds.

In the pond dead moths could be seen floating amidst scum.

DRINKING ALONE AND PONDERING ON THE PRIMEVAL FLUID. THE GREAT BEGINNING. SUN. MOON. STARS. SUSPENDED IN THE SKY. A JADE IMMORTAL TRIED TO PAWN A CORNER OF THE HEAVENS FOR A SACK OF RICE BUT WAS UNSUCCESSFUL. WARY OF DRINKING FROM THE BIG DIPPER.

Nocturnal
tree limbs,
dull clouds,
strange sounds.
In darkness
moonbeams,
cold smiles,
shivering.
Silhouettes,
sharp shapes,
nighttime
masquerade.
In darkness
tree limbs
so black
shivering.

A man chews shallots while watching plum petals in a
puddle.

Exposed and transparent,
my tears mingle with the stream.

He couldn't cut a persimmon with a fifteen-foot spear.

A discerning fellow would say, "Pi Wei stealing the wine was a case of filial piety. But how can one rate such a thing? Should he be despised for his conduct, or praised for it?"

Master T'uan taught him Heavenly Plum Style.

"Feet and hands move together," he said. "Lunging and blocking—like writing poetry with a brush. A snake strikes with its poisonous fangs; a crane attacks with its beak; a tiger uses its claws. The heel of the hand is stronger than the knuckles of the fist. Some talk of external and internal kung fu—but such talk is like the blabbering of a precocious child. Skin without bones or bones without skin—both would mean that you are a dead man. Does the wing of a dragonfly have an in or an out? When the wind blows, the clouds flee. If you slap someone, they're bound to know it. Knowing it, they'll react. One wades in the river to get to the other bank—but suddenly you're a thousand miles downstream!"

Pi Wei was made to do squatting drills.

"If someone is near you, use your elbow like this . . ."

"Like this?"

"Right, but you have to be careful. You could kill a man that way!"

"Oh . . ."

"Your hands should move around like birds or butterflies—don't be a drag. The worst possible thing in martial arts is to be clumsy! . . . Have to be both swift and grounded, light and heavy."

Pi Wei lunged towards the sun, ducked towards the ground, pivoted this way and that, repeating the complicated moves the master had shown him.

"No—not like that! Your feet look like sinking boats!"

He tried again.

"No!"

He tried again.

"**No!**"

"But Master . . ."

"Here, let me give you some secret transmission."

A smack to the head.

"Master!"

"Don't be stupid. Keep trying. Practice makes perfect. If you don't maintain your center, you won't have ch'i. If your body is tilted this way and that, your ch'i will be scattered. If your ch'i is scattered, how can you expect your blows and kicks to have strength? If your blows and kicks don't have strength, you might land ten thousand, but still not even be able to scratch dew."

The master lifted a cup full of wine to his lips and Pi Wei bowed deeply.

23.

"Why do you wish to learn kung fu?"

"The tax collector Eunuch Sung killed my father, so I wish to . . ."

"Bad idea."

"But . . . ?"

"Just try to stay out of trouble! And more wine. I'm running low."

> The mountain valley is mounting the giant
> vegetation;
> for profound jade, brave glens sparkle;
> when sod acts, the master soaks the guest;
> it is spitting, startled incessantly.

Pi Wei's sleeping place was on the porch. He lay awake, listening to the wind.

He would leave the floating cash on a rock, with a few light branches over it, so it would have to work itself out before coming back.

24.

Since Master T'uan did not know that the wine was stashed in a nearby cave, every time Pi Wei went to fetch some, he had to claim that he was getting it from Two Wells Village, which meant that he always had some time to kill. He would usually do some training while waiting for the appropriate moment to return.

On metal snake day, however, he had a sudden desire to see his mother. It had been a great while since he had been put out on his own and he had thought about her often. She probably regretted her action—shed tears for him and wished he would return—wished he would pay her visits and comfort her.

He went to Liulin, and then made his way to the old neighborhood. It had changed.

His old house had been bought by a butcher, but the butcher had since sold it to a music instructor. From the street Pi Wei could hear the sound of the ku-ch'in.

Other houses in the neighborhood had, it seemed, been bought by wealthier folks and there were several new buildings that looked as if they had cost a good deal to erect.

The lanes in that neighborhood used to be quite dirty, but now they seemed neat. Peddlers used to wander through the area shouting out their wares—but he didn't see any now. There used to be chickens in the street—but those too had disappeared.

The changes made him feel sad, as if his childhood too had disappeared.

The outside of Mr. Yu's house had been done up. There was a wooden gate with an inscribed plaque above it that read:

Happy hearts make a happy home.

He approached the door and knocked. A bitchy-looking servant answered.

"What do you want?"

"I'm here to see . . ."

"Huh?"

"Madame . . . Yi'an."

"She's busy. What's up?"

"I . . . I . . ."

"Who's that?" came a voice from behind the servant.

Then Pi Wei saw his mother.

She was dressed in a pink gown and her face was covered in rice powder. She was standing before Pi Wei. A strong scent of bitter orange came from her person. Her lips were pressed tightly together and her eyes scanned the form of her son, down and up, up and down.

She seemed to hesitate for a moment about what to do, but then invited him in. The servant raised her eyebrows and pouted. She wondered who the lad was,

88

but wasn't about to ask questions—if Madame wanted to invite dirty young men back into her chamber, that was her business.

She led Pei Wei back to her room and served him some lukewarm tea, from a pot that she had already been drinking. Pei Wei looked around. His mother was certainly living in better style than she had with his father. There was a little table laden with combs, perfumes and make-up. There was an illustrated book of pornography open on the floor. Madame Yi'an saw that it attracted her son's eyes, so shut it and smiled uneasily.

She considered asking her servant to bring in some snacks, but then decided against it—she didn't want the interview to last too long. She asked Pi Wei what had prompted the visit.

"Mother . . ."

"Mhm?"

"I . . . I think of you."

"It's only natural," she said after a pause.

"And father."

"Right."

"Mother . . . I am learning kung fu!"

"Don't talk nonsense. I heard you were working at a wine shop, taking care of the toilet."

"Yes, but . . ."

Pi Wei was hesitant to tell his mother that he was no longer working at the wine shop. From the tone of her voice it seemed she was somewhat proud that her son was gainfully employed, so how could he tell her the truth?

"Mr. Yu loves wine," she continued. "He drinks a few carafes every night. He especially likes the good stuff— but it's awfully pricey."

"Mother, I am going to avenge father. Every day I practice boxing. Eunuch Sung is going to pay for his crime!"

Madame Yi'an gazed up at the ceiling. "You're so stubborn!" she said.

Pi Wei looked at his mother with sadness. Had she not loved his father at all, then?

"Do you get an employee discount?"

"Discount?"

"The wine. If you could get us a few pecks of Yellow Rose Essence at a reasonable price, it might be worth it."

When Pi Wei walked away from his mother's residence he felt extremely forlorn—like someone woken from a beautiful dream by the sound of mallets breaking down a wall. A cloud drifted in front of the sun. A woman at her doorstep gave him an unfriendly look. He noticed a gang of young men formed near a tea stall. As he passed them by, he looked one in the face and recognized Shih-tseng, one of the boys who used to harass him.

"Hey, isn't that . . . ?" the lad said.

"It's Pi Wei!"

"That little cunt we used to kick around!"

The gang all ran up around him. Since Pi Wei had left the neighborhood years before, they had never been able to find anyone who was as much fun to pick on. They all had fond memories of calling him names and chasing him.

"He looks almost exactly the same!" one of the fellows said.

"Smells just as bad!" said another.

Shih-tseng shoved his grinning face up to Pi Wei so the latter could smell his breath, which was like rotting meat.

Pi Wei was filled with sudden anger—anger at them, his mother, Eunuch Sung, the world! He shoved his palm into Shih-tseng's face, and the nose of the latter flattened into a bloody patch.

"Ow! Ow! Ow!"

"That bastard just hurt Shih-tseng!"

"Let's get him!"

They all jumped on Pi Wei at once. One grabbed him from behind while another punched him in the stomach. They began to beat and kick him. He tried to avoid blows, to block them, to deliver his own, but there were so many arms and legs coming at him at once that he became confused.

When Pi Wei got back to Master T'uan's place, bruised and disheveled, the latter clicked his tongue and looked at the young man in disgust.

"There were five of them," Pi Wei said, by way of excuse.

"So you thought no one but you lived in the world and if trouble came along you'd be boxing with your own shadow? It seems I have been given a very dull-witted student."

"But . . . Master . . ."

Master T'uan shook his head. "It isn't easy to get good at boxing," he said, lifting the wine cup to his lips and taking a sip. "It is like growing a garden. It isn't enough to have a good piece of land. You need good seeds and to plant them at the right time. If you plant snow peas too late, they will deteriorate before they gain proper vigor. If you plant eggplants when the soil is too cold, they won't germinate. It is the same with boxing. Every technique has to be learned at the right time. Should one learn charioteering before learning how to ride a horse or learn mathematics before one can count to ten? It's lucky for you that I've had pity on you. There are many false adepts in the world. Some will claim that they will teach you all sorts of techniques, but they themselves do not even know how to stand properly. Others have knowledge, but are parsimonious about sharing it. Most teachers would be asking high fees or for you to go off and kill somebody for them. The only reason I bother showing you a few things is because you're so pathetic. But that quality will only get you so far. Silly laughter is charming in a sixteen-year-old lass, but becomes a real fault in a sixty-year-old matron. When a child pouts, it is adorable, but the same action is treated with contempt when done by a grown man. That is why all things have their season. In winter one conserves one's energy, because at that time the *yin* is absolute, but in spring flashes of thunder fill the sky and *yang* appears. Soon the oriole sounds its flute and the dove begins to coo. The farmers watch as sprouts emerge from their fields and the bear emerges from its cave. You need to change your attitude. The attitude can be changed through practice. Practice makes perfect. These days students expect to gain skill without repetition. They stretch their arms and legs for a few minutes in the courtyard of their mansions and call it training, or waddle around in the mud and call it rigorous preparation for the great event. Martial arts have become corrupt, and the only people who seem to practice them are thugs and eunuchs. They are performed without grace or talent. A good boxer can defeat a bad one by just touching him with a feather. The trick is to discover the opponent's shortcomings. The hawk can fly high, but is useless underground. A serpent poses danger to feet and legs, but can do no harm if one is soaring in the clouds. Some men pride themselves on their daring, but often get restless. Others pride themselves on their cunning, but often hesitate at the critical juncture. One needn't dig a big hole to catch a small dog. After a large meal, a man has trouble walking half a *li*. Not eating for a week, a beggar can barely stand on his two feet. Half empty, half full—a vessel that is neither overflowing nor gathering dust—only acting so can one manage at the decisive moment to keep from falling into a precipice."

The humiliation Pi Wei had received made him double down on his training. His eight hours a day turned into twelve, but then, thinking about how those lads had beat him up, and remembering his father dying in the road, he increased it to eighteen. When the sun left at dusk, he would be training, and when it returned at dawn, he would be training.

"Did he even go to sleep?" it would ask itself.

25.

Training schedule:

Hour of the tiger: Wake up. Drink decoction of atractylodes rhizome and honey-fried licorice root. Go to the east office. Little Chariot.

Hour of the rabbit: Practice Eight Sections Brocade.

Hour of the dragon: Bowl of gruel; meditation on the big emptiness.

Hour of the snake: Practice Nine Rotations and then the first form, called "Tyrant Tosses the Iron Bell."

Hour of the horse: Lunch on millet and mountain herbs. Tidy the place up. Chop wood.

Hour of the goat: Practice second form, called "Rhinoceros Gazes at the Moon."

Hour of the monkey: Practice third form, called "Thirty-two Maneuver Long Strikes to Route out Ghosts."

Hour of the rooster: Supper of millet and quick-boiled lamb's quarters.

Hour of the dog: Practice Willful Fist.

Hour of the pig: To sleep already!

26.

GHOSTS STRIDE ALONG THE PATHS OF THE
WORLD OF DUST HUNGRY FOR YOUR BLOOD
MONSTERS WISHING TO CRUSH YOUR BONES.
MOVE YOUR BODY; STILL YOUR MIND.
EXCEEDINGLY ANCIENT SPARRING STYLE.
WHITE LIGHT REFLECTED ON SLITHERING
BROOKS.
(hands are two traps to catch falling stars
(the original nature of your opponent
(revolve around him like the sun around a peak
(vibrating palm and swaying leaves

    The master hit him. THE MASTER HIT HIM. **THE
MASTER HIT HIM!**

Standing dragon tiger claw
Thrusting fingers, pounding fists
Chopping exercise, backfist drill

**HARDNESS MUST BE USED!
SOFTNESS MUST BE USED!**

Pi Wei was made to stand on one leg for several days. Every once in a while Master T'uan would walk by and give him a look of disapproval.

SIXTY THOUSAND PIGMIES WERE BORN FROM THE HAIR OF THE GODDESS, BUT HAS ONE PURE THOUGHT EVER BEEN BORN IN YOUR HEAD?

"You're in lousy shape," Master T'uan said.

Tso Tz'u slept and ate at the same time. Ch'ien Lou put on a cloak of sunbeams. Master T'uan swallowed rice wine and staggered. Pi Wei struck at the wind and shed tears of exasperation.

"You really are a bad student!" the master said, and then proceeded to beat him up.

The master tossed him here and there. Flung him over his shoulder, tripped him, flipped him, pushed him, pulled him. Sometimes he went ten feet high and landed with a thud on the ground. Getting up, dizzy, he was tossed to the west. Struggling to his feet, eyeballs bobbing about, he was flung to the east.

Boxing with the clouds.

"Some branches bend, others remain firm," Master T'uan said. "The tips of the branches of a plum tree are like arrows and are aligned with the eight trigrams; the flowers have eight faces. The branches all grow in the same direction, supported by the trunk, but not causing it anguish. The blossoms are the *yang*, the trunk and branches the *yin*. The blossoms are tranquil as a third daughter, the trunk as rousing as a first son. Even bandits will be pacified by a third daughter. Even demons will quit hurling evil when confronted by a first son."

27.

"Master . . . how am I doing?"

"So-so."

"Am I not almost there?"

"Not even halfway."

"But . . ."

"Keep trying. Practice makes perfect."

"Your hands are still too soft."

"But Master!"

Master T'uan picked up a rock and ground it to dust in his palm.

"When you can do this, your hands will be hard enough," he said.

"And how?"

"Iron-palm formula and a bit of training. Practice makes perfect!"

Master T'uan showed him how to make iron-palm formula from: pyrite, good for bones; safflower, to invigorate circulation; acanthopanax root bark, to keep the hands from swelling; ground-up skeletal fossil of the mastodon, to calm skeletal muscles; sappan wood, to invigorate the blood; clematis, to lessen pain; dried and ground white flower snake, to relax tensions; mastic, to repair muscles; wingless cockroaches, to strengthen bones and muscles; trichosanthes seeds, help facilitate healing; flying squirrel feces, to prevent muscle spasms; angelica root tail, to prevent inflammation; dipascus root, to relieve pain; dragon blood, to heal; peach kernels, to inhibit pain; akebia promotes blood circulation; cinnamon twigs, for expelling dampness; white dahlia root, for its tonic effect; pseudoginseng, in order to reduce tenderness; costus root, to cleanse the palms; notopterygium root, to tame muscle spasms; *Saposhnikovia divaricata* root, for expelling wind; tinospora stem, for its anti-inflammatory effect; dried rhizomes of bugleweed, to reduce swelling in the joints and promote the circulation of blood and energy.

Pi Wei punched weeds, then sand, then rocks.

"The rocks are hard, they hurt my hands!"

"Tough luck!"

"Maybe I could hit a tree?"

"No!"

Hit bag filled with mung beans fifty times a day. Hit bag filled with mung beans seventy-five times a day. Hit bag filled with mung beans one hundred times a day. Hit bag filled with mung beans two hundred times a day. Hit bag filled with mung beans five hundred times a day. Bare knuckle and fingertip pushups! Chop and claw! Switch from beans to pebbles! Switch to half pebbles, half iron shot! Switch to all iron shot!

Every day his body became less soft. His waist had been like congealed pig's fat, but was now like river-washed stones. The chords of his neck looked like they could be used to tie up bandits or tigers.

"Should I keep hitting the iron shot?"
"Yes! Practice makes perfect!"

Advanced training: cauldron full of sand over a hot fire—submerging and then retracting open palms. A ghost-echo from a far off country.

"Stick out your hands."
When Pi Wei did so, Master T'uan struck them savagely with a length of split bamboo. Pi Wei giggled.
"Good, now your hands can feel no pain."

"How am I doing, Master?"
"Still a neophyte. Keep trying. Practice makes perfect."

28.

Summer faded away and fall came. A thousand peaks blushed, all confronted by the same dilemma—then covered themselves with clouds, and rain fell, drops making spiders' webs more visible. Pi Wei would strip himself down to the waist and train as slanting drops struck against his face and chest. Master T'uan sat in his hut, half-drunk, regulating his cup, letting his roots flourish, his mind on the Tao. Fall turned to winter. Pi Wei stood on one leg in the cold. His body became dusted with snow—but his mind maintained its focus. Ice formed over the creek. Walking over the two-log bridge, he could hear the water murmuring beneath. The master had him heat his wine and treated him terribly—certainly worse than Mr. and Mrs. Wang at the wine shop or his mother had ever treated him—called him unpleasant names, hit him, put under countless tortures and trials. But Master T'uan taught him, so, for Pi Wei, he was as great as heaven itself.

He, every day, thought of Eunuch Sung and his poor father, who had been killed by the former for no good reason—just for getting a little night soil on him. He remembered how his father, though poor and simple, had always cared for him. When his mother scolded him, he would always take the boy's side.

And he recalled the day he had died. His poor bloodied frame. He remembered how someone had come and covered the body with a sedge mat and then it was carried away. The last thing he saw of his father was his feet. One of them was without a sandal. He had looked around for it, but couldn't find it.

Thinking thus, Pi Wei fortified himself for revenge.

When spring again came, the world was full of the songs of birds. The green mountains looked like folded brocade. The rivers glittered in the sun. Pi Wei felt a great joy within him. When he practiced punches, his fists made a swishing sound.

HU! HA! HU! was the sound he would make when training.

29.

Master T'uan would only have sex with trees, but would never consummate the act. In this way he reached for the moon, while stroking the stars. His lovers were pines. His lovers were three-flowered maples. His lovers were chestnuts. All stood waiting, available when he wished—they dreamt slow dreams of his embrace—being massaged by his strong hands—beard against bark—lips against trunk.

Embracing them, he gained power. Licking them, he gained strength. He licked the sap from their crevices and sucked the juice from their leaves—nibbled on their twigs and rubbed against their bark.

This was a practice he hadn't talked to Pi Wei about. Some men are discreet.

One day, however, he decided his student was ready.

"You've made some headway with your fists, but your ch'i is still pretty so-so."

"So-so?"

The master frowned and nodded his head.

"How can I improve it, Master?" Pi Wei asked.

"Sex with trees. A practice handed down from teacher to student for quite some time. But a fellow like you . . ."

"A fellow like me?"

"Probably not suited."

"So?"

"It's pretty hard to advance."

"Oh . . ."

"Mmmhm."

Pi Wei became decidedly uneasy. "But Master . . ." he murmured.

Master T'uan pointed towards the forest. "Go down there and see what you can find."

"A tree?"

Master T'uan clicked his tongue and gave Pi Wei a look of disapproval. Was his student really so witless?

Pi Wei wandered towards the forest, feeling extremely awkward. It was early spring, and he crossed the meadow, his sandaled feet brushing against first flowers in bloom. A single butterfly floated by, seeming lost. A bee murmured morning prayers as it sailed over tender grass.

He was soon enveloped in the shade of the trees. The heady smell of pine filled his nose. A starling screeched high up on a branch. A breeze came and brushed through the boughs above, making them whisper.

He moved slowly, warily. He heard a stick crack and jumped, thinking it might be a wild animal—but it was a jay rooting around on the forest floor. He heard a high-pitched frenetic sound and looked over. There was a small, perfectly formed hole in a tree trunk from which the sound came. Was it a woodpecker's nest?

In truth, having grown up in the city, primitive nature made him feel somewhat uncomfortable. When he smiled, the trees and rocks just stared at him. When he greeted a chipmunk, the latter just made a nonsensical noise. He looked about at the trees and juxtaposed them with the ladies he had seen on Better Than Home Lane—and by comparison, the latter seemed infinitely more accessible—for the ladies of the lane all had mouths and smiles and swelling breasts and bobbing heads and he had seen how they would grab men's hands and drag the fellows in, fan themselves and cast longing glances, ready to do it and do it all—make the yellow stream flow, sport beneath the red candles, peck at the crimson bird and let the hair needles drop.

The blue pines, standing stately and staring down at him, made him feel his low-born status, his mud-splashed mind. Was he really comparing them to ladies of the pleasure quarters?

"They might not want to be embraced by one like me," he thought.

There was a maple, but it seemed rather small for his purposes. There was a cypress, but it seemed too large—his arms could never fit around it. The smaller pines all had sharp, low-hanging branches. He couldn't have grasped one without impaling himself—the larger had bark that was rather rough and conveyed to him a sense of uncertainty.

"I will just return and tell the Master that I have performed sex with trees. How will he know the difference?"

Just then, however, a breeze blew through the forest and a nearby branch swayed. Pi Wei looked up.

It stood there, seeming to blossom shyly. He approached and its leaves trembled. At the base of its trunk grew thick moss, but higher up there was none. He put his hand there. The bark was cool and pleasant to the touch.

"Hello . . ."

Something profound; a galloping horse was his heart.

He affixed his lips to its trunk.

At first the tree seemed resistant. Though standing still, to Pi Wei, it seemed as if it were trying to turn away. He was somewhat confused and pulled back.

"Ah, excuse me," he said. "I . . . I didn't know."

Its branches were like phoenix-tails; its every aspect full of luxuriant fascination. It was modest as a mountain temple half hidden in mist or a glance reflected in a stream. He found a grotto in her trunk and pushed himself against it. Agitated himself like waves slapping against the shore—his fingers clambered up and down like crabs over sand

drifting

drifting

drifting

soaring

soaring

soaring

tremble and cry

cry and tremble

eeeeeee!

ahhhhh!

ooooo!

mmmmmmmmmmmmmmm

nnnnnnnn

floating

floating.

And so it was that their fates became interwoven.

Pi Wei wondered why he had not come to the forest before.

The next day Master T'uan tossed a tattered old book at him.

"Read that . . . but just the first part. Leave the inner chapters alone."

30.

Mysterious Scripture of Tree Sex
Inscribed by the Worthy of the Big Dipper
[Extracts]

After dining on icicles and red berries, the sage-infant Grand Clarity descended to the Yellow Dusk Forest and for ninety years sought the secret of pacing the void. Having had countless relationships with trees—with Manchurian ash and paperback maple, with white oak and three-needled pine, with weeping torreya and weeping willow—he took the excretion of his experience and put it as follows:

There are three types of sex with trees. Some practice only the little sex, called Small Boy's Method of Sex with Trees. To do this, one should proceed with reverence, discard assumptions, move forward like a paint-powdered butterfly. For beginning students, nothing is more important. The needs of men and trees are not equal. The energy of man is intense, while that of trees, dormant. The energy of a man is short; that of a tree, long. Learning to regulate his desires by the temporal measures of a tree, man fortifies his ch'i.

○

If you wish to eat pine needles for a million years, you had better form family bonds with the pine. That gnarled tree that no ax would care to touch—what hidden beauties might it not have in its heart?

○

Lovers make all sorts of sounds, but the most appropriate is *hsü*.

○

Love between a man and woman occurs in the postnatal realm; the love of trees, in the prenatal. The prenatal realm is the origin. Without knowing their origins, men wander through the world like lost ghosts. Lucidity is key.

○

Stick your head into the green depths of a sky-touching tree—it has been growing for four thousand seasons. Its roots are deep, so why would it fall when you grapple with it?

○

Seekers of immortality wander from mountain to mountain searching out rock excrescences and longevity water.

They nibble on mushrooms and lichens and gather up cinnabar and laminar malachite, hoping thereby to gain fullness of life. And yet, all the while, they pass through forests and ignore countless trees, each of which could bestow the secret of immortality. What irony!

○

The second type of sex with trees is called Congress of the Boiling Heaven. In it, the man clings to the tree as if he were a vine. He holds close, as if he wished to enter directly into the trunk. Biting the bark, he gains potency. Clinging to the foliage, he harmonizes with Mars and enters into sagehood. It is like the awakening of a heron. When a heron awakes, it flaps its wings. Flapping its wings, it can stir the wind or soar up high.

○

Men are full of base desires. Only through wood can they be properly trained. Can eternity be attained by handling short-lived things?

○

Though any season will do, the best time to begin practice is in the spring, facing east.

○

Exhale and inhale, go now fast, now slow. Let fingertips and spine move as one.

No need to hurry. A session should last from the hour of the rabbit to the hour of the dragon; from the hour of the snake to the hour of the goat. Wander along the mountain paths of sex with trees, linger in its meadows, admiring the beauty of the scenery—the distant peaks and peaceful grottos, spring hills and luminous clearings.

Some are worried about hard and soft, but that is not the way of the Congress of the Boiling Heaven. When two stones are rubbed together, out fly heavenly sparks. When conducting sex with trees, one is conducting an athletic endeavor. The practitioner pants as if he were running forty *li*; he grunts as if he were lifting two hundred *jin*.

Grand Clarity said: The longevity of the pine is noteworthy. Sharing its love, how could it not share its essence with you? The beauty of the birch rivals that of the moon, so how could it not surpass that of mortal women? Its leaves carry with them the ripple of the ocean and the refinement of stars; its roots curl like dragons and spread like clouds. Becoming intimate with it, one will soar like a falcon and fly like the wind. Even Confucius instructed his pupils beneath a ginkgo tree. Imagine if he had had the wisdom to have sex with it and pass this talent on to the world? The tree stands, waiting for insemination. By tempting it, the most arcane principles are learned; by enticing it, the mysteries of heaven and earth appear in the palm of one's hand. No wonder it is called Eyes of the Cosmic Spirit!

○

The third type is the consummate sex called Black Dragon Swinging its Tail, but the dangers of practicing it are great. It is like stretching the waning moon to make it full again. When the moon is full, the lunar essence is swallowed. When the lunar essence is swallowed, the vacuous grotto is filled. When the vacuous grotto is filled, luminescence is attained.

○

When fluid is retained, it is *yin*. When fluid is lost, it is *yang*. The wooden boat floats on the *yin* fluid. The metal raft sinks in the *yang* fluid. When you agitate your body, the earth shudders. Left and right, forward and backward. This is called kinetic energy.

○

By dispensing with mortal sex, and only engaging in sex with trees, the sage travels a thousand *li* with just one stride.

○

But then what are the dangers? Practicing this method, the teeth of the white tiger are loosened. The eagles drift away, and take their protecting talons elsewhere. The glass is emptied. When liquid is spilled, it always runs downward. Who ever heard of a river flowing up a mountain? The venerable gods weep and hide their eyes with their sleeves. A great sage, when empty, is full; when low, is high. But this isn't something for the average mortal. And so it is that while most sink in emptiness, a few might float.

As Wu Wen said to Ts'ai Tan, "All men are not boats."

○

Interlocutor. With my head buried in the sack of Confucianism, I am unable to see the world around me. What should I do?

Grand Clarity. Living in an age of confusion, it is difficult for people to discern the true from the false. People take poisons, mistaking them for elixirs of longevity. They disdain thistle and mercury, though they have healthful benefits. People enter forests, chop down the trees, and burn the wood, little suspecting that they are killing their own wives and concubines. It is like trying to sweep away the North Star, mistaking it for a spider. Not drinking water, one gets thirsty. Not sleeping, one gets tired. Only fools deny things that are universally true.

Interlocutor. I have been practicing astrology, numerology and spirit writing for a great many years, yet still have not gained insight. Is there a better way?

Grand Clarity. The arts you have been practicing have their place in the world of dust, but amongst immortals they are all considered quite useless. The best thing is to practice sex with trees, and forget the numerous arts, the Six Classics, and the five phases.

Interlocutor. The Taoist classics say that practicing sex with women shortens one's lifespan. I fear that if I practice sex with trees the situation will be even worse. Is this true?

Grand Clarity. It is common knowledge that the Yellow Emperor had a harem of one thousand two hundred, but what few understand is that these were not mortal women but trees. How else could he have lived to the ripe old age of three hundred and ninety-seven? Wi Fu spent many years having sex with weeds and lived through more than one hundred springs and autumns. How much longer would he have lived if he had had sex with ancient pines that rise one hundred feet in the air? Sheng Chung-shan lived on Horse Mane Mountain and took a lacquer tree for a wife. It is said he lived through three dynasties. Chang Tzu-ts'ung lived near the marshes and was intimate with a chestnut and his hair was still black at the age of one hundred and three. Lü Shang, despised by his wife, abandoned the world and lived a quiet life fishing and practicing sex with a crab apple tree by the name of Green Girl, before, at the age of one hundred and eighty, King Wen of Zhou discovered him and made him prime minister. Peng Zu lived to be eight hundred and of his eight disciples, none lived to be less than two hundred. The reason for this is that he bestowed on them the recipe for sex with trees.

Interlocutor. You say that there are three methods of sex with trees, but declare that the third is dangerous to practice, so why bother mentioning it?

Grand Clarity. There are many types of men. Some are small, some are medium, and a very few are great. Though there are many soldiers, does that mean one should not bring wine to the general? Though there are several generals, does that mean that the king should not be fed? Each man must adapt himself to the correct sexual procedures for his station. But, just because the king is sleeping, it does not mean that the cupbearer should secretly sit on the throne. Just because there exists such a thing as a fly, does that mean we should not have eyes for the phoenix?

31.

This constant dream.

Standing, arms outstretched. My companions—birds building nests between my fingers, spiders' webs in my hair, spirits drifting past me. Summer night, winter night, spring night. When he put his lips to me for the first time, I did not know what that was. He grabbed me and held me. When I stood under the foot of the sun, I quietly felt. At first it was uncomfortable. Then it was the most beautiful. The most beautiful. The most beautiful moon came out that night after he had left me with his heart. Most beautiful body for me. Soft whispers. Really a good young man! His skin is so pure! He let me own! Does he desire my bark so much? We are one. I am the most beautiful tree in the forest? When the east wind blew through my leaves, I sang low. Birds flew by and squirrels ran down to my legs. Away with you insect voices, I only want to hear him, feel him against me like a big snail!

32.

And so it was that, with that tree, he devoured the twilight and drank the sunrise and, day by day, his ch'i grew stronger. Not consummating the act, restraining himself, water never met wood—instead nurturing his own inner being—feeding his secret pools. It was as if he were extracting clouds from heaven and setting them beneath his feet, and so his feet, floating on lightness, became excessively nimble. It was as if he were pulling chunks of iron ore from beneath the ground and planting them in his fists, and so his fists, gaining in weight, became excessively strong.

When he trained, his fists sang through the air, cutting it swiftly. In a stance, his feet seemed as if sealed to the ground.

He used the iron-palm formula, and could chop soft rocks in two.

Master T'uan sparred with him a bit and saw that his balance was good. He nodded his head in approval.

"That's fine," he said. "Keep embracing the trees."

Pi Wei had never felt this way before. While training, his mind kept wandering back to the tree. He thought of its branches, how they stretched up towards the sky. He thought of its trunk, how it sloped down to the earth. Embracing it was like embracing creation. He felt like an orphan who had found a home, a wounded animal who was cared for, a door that had just been opened.

Tremblingly he put his arms around it. He had never realized how smooth bark could be. He wished he could merge with it, like salt with water or minutes with time.

The wind, as it breathed through the tree's branches, made a *shuuu shuuu* sound.

"Oh, Susu," he said, giving her a name.

At night, he had difficulty sleeping, thinking of that breeze playing with her branches. He would drink his morning tea nervously, and had lost the taste for his mid-day millet.

One night he had a dream:

Clouds swimming swiftly through the sky.

Echo of the wind. Wandering through high grass. A hill. A woman stands alone. Her arms are outstretched, fingers splayed. She is wearing a green gown that flaps in the moving air. And her hair is undone and churns about like seaweed in a current. Her eyes are closed.

"The wind is always pushing me around," she says, in a voice full of sadness.

"Who are you?" he asks.

"You don't recognize me?"

"Oh! Oh! You . . . you . . ."

"You keep embracing me, but why won't you make me yours? We could have children together—but would they be able to walk, or would they stand firm like me? Oh, dear, please nurture my desires!"

"But, I can't!"

"I have to wait for rain?"

33.

"Master, the grain is all gone!"

"Grain?"

"Millet. Rice. Sorghum. No grain!"

The old man clicked his tongue. "Addicted to grain, your energy slips away. Captivated by starches, your ch'i is like tea cast in a sieve."

"Master, you never eat food!"

"I can go a year without eating food, but a day without drinking wine makes me grouchy."

"But, Master, for this useless student it's hard to embrace the tree—it's hard to train on an empty belly."

"These younglings . . ."

"Master . . ."

"What happened to the beans?"

"I ate them!"

Master T'uan looked at his student with disapproval, then looked at the wine jar. There wasn't much liquid left.

"Here, you can borrow some of my floating cash," he said. "But get me some alcohol down there at Two Wells Village while you're at it."

Pi Wei grabbed up the buckets and yoke and went off. In the spring sunshine the water of the creek looked just like fat. Beyond the sound of a cool wind, a bird call could be heard faintly.

He left the buckets on the side of the trail, near where the wine was stashed away. He would get it on the way back.

Two Wells Village! Two Wells Village! He had never been to Two Wells Village. Would he ever go?

It was towards Liulin that his legs carried him and he thought he would get himself some lunch while he was there. He hadn't eaten meat in a great while—and with the floating cash it wouldn't be a problem to get himself a healthy taste. So, after purchasing a sack of millet to bring back to the mountains, he went to a restaurant in the market and ordered a bowl of rice, some roasted pork, and chicken feet in black bean sauce.

The pork was slightly crisp on the outside, and very tender and succulent inside—a little sweet, with a tangy insistence, like a host offering innumerable gifts. Its surface glistened like sea waves in the sun. Bits of lean and bits of fat made it delicious. The chicken feet were wonderful—like braised phoenix claws, plump morsels of meat falling right off the bone and tendon as if of their own will. The taste was lush as a field in summer, as clear as a mountain shallow in spring.

Pi Wei's chopsticks kept going out for more—travelling from the food to his mouth with great alacrity.

Looking up, he saw a group of men strolling through the market with big strides—grabbing things and not paying; scowling as if they were tasting something sour; sneering; picking their noses; swaying their shoulders and hips as they walked. There were half a dozen of them, but two, by their mannerisms, and the fancy silk sashes they wore around their waists, were obviously the senior members of the gang. One of them had a thick beard that hung all the way down his chest. He was big, with ox-like eyes and an enormous nose with flaring nostrils. His name was Purple Bearded Meng-fu. The other was short and fit with a thick mane of well-combed hair. This fellow's name was Wild Ch'ing-t'ung. When he walked, he bent his knees much more than most men do, lending his gate an unusual swagger.

When they came to a shop opposite the restaurant—a place that sold women's hairpins and accoutrements—they started hassling the owner—giving him a shake-down—snatching up beauty items for their lady friends and demanding cash for their boss.

"It's those bastards of Eunuch Sung's," he heard one of the men at another table say in a low voice to his companion.

"Just don't look and eat your soup. What can low ones like us do about anything?"

Pi Wei swallowed down the rest of his food as fast as he could, plopped a few coins on the table, and, grabbing his sack of millet, followed the roughs. As they went along, they did the same thing, hassling shop owners and getting money and free gifts.

Finally, when they were at the east end of the market, which was less crowded, Pi Wei approached them.

"Hey," he said, "aren't you fellows from Eunuch Sung's group?"

"And if we are what the hell is it to you?" Wild Ch'ing-t'ung replied.

"Oh, my father had a debt to pay him before he passed away and so I'm always looking for an opportunity to do this in his place."

Ch'ing-t'ung gazed high and low at Pi Wei and put on a frowning expression. He saw something unadorned in every way, worn sandals, old trousers.

"You look pretty poor to me," he said. "How the hell could you pay back any outstanding debts?"

"Well, I may not have money, but I have my hands."

"Hands?"

Pi Wei dropped the sack of millet and his palms whistled through the air as he performed a bit of his Tyrant Tosses the Iron Bell routine.

Purple Bearded Meng-fu laughed. "That little fucker wants a piece of you," he said to Ch'ing-t'ung.

Ch'ing-t'ung swung his fist at Pi Wei, but the latter stepped aside. Pi Wei's fists went out, pitter-patted on Ch'ing-t'ung's face, and half a second later there was nothing there but a sore, bloody pancake with two eyes staring out of it in wonder.

"Worthless spinule!" one of the other men cried, and threw himself forward.

He was one of those fighters who was all about the legs. His foot shot towards Pi Wei's mid-section, but the violence was parried. Mr. Legs swung his heel at Pi Wei's head, but the latter pulled it back, staring at the foot like one slightly offended at an off-color remark. A moment later Mr. Legs was flying through the air like a wind-borne fragrance.

A number of people now stood around and were looking, pointing, making comments. When Pi Wei landed a blow they would smile. A few laughs were heard. It was clear they had no sympathy for Eunuch Sung's gang.

A salve and ointment seller in the crowd nodded his head in delight. As things were going, there would be a good demand for his black ghost pain relieving lotion.

There were four bad actors left: Purple Bearded Meng-fu and three bit players. The latter attacked at once, under the theory that six fists beat two. Pi Wei was at first driven back a bit, but then, collecting himself, landed a strike on the face of one, who immediately gave in. The other two came lunging at Pi Wei at once and the youth cartwheeled out of the way, so that their blows only struck nothingness. One tried to wreck Pi Wei's knee-cap with his foot, but the son of Jung flipped up and over, landed in a prone position with his hands palms down under his shoulders, his back straight, and the balls of his feet on the ground, and then sprang ten feet into the air. When he descended, one foot went east, the other west; one crunching a jaw, the other smashing some features.

Even though his companions had all been beaten, Meng-fu stepped forward with confidence. He had been getting in brawls since before he could remember, and had never been bettered in a fight. He clenched his hands into fists and then spit on the ground.

Meng-fu was not an especially fast fighter, but he was quite strong, and his strikes were hard. Pi Wei eluded the first few blows, but then caught one on the right side of his chest and realized that he had best be careful. He dodged and darted, shifted and bobbed, with such alacrity that Meng-fu became confused. Seeing his opportunity, Pi Wei landed a devil's kick square in the face of his antagonist, causing blood.

A few of the bystanders made "wow" sounds. Someone chuckled.

Meng-fu's face became heated. He cast off all caution and rushed at Pi Wei, his fists crushing the air. The young man avoided one blow and wiped aside another, and then, as delicately as a heron testing the waters of Ever-calm Pool, toed Meng-fu right between the legs, and when the hands of the latter descended to retrieve the stolen jewels, the hands of the former knocked him on the nose, swatted him on the cheek, and pecked him in the eye.

> High up on Myriad Prospects Cliff
> sit fragile eggs
> which if broken
> will make
> the mother bird cry.
> When a nest is shorn of its eggs
> can it still be called a nest?

Purple Bearded Meng-fu was in great pain. He was in great pain and furious. He was furious and in great pain. Everyone was looking and he felt humiliated. The whole reason he had become a thug in the first place was to avoid such situations—to have people fear him and kowtow to him—not the very opposite!

34.

Eunuch Sung prayed fervently to Ts'ai Shen, the god of wealth. It wasn't that he needed more money, so much as the fact that he *wanted* more.

Ts'ai Shen, having excellent hearing, heard his prayers, but found them rather irritating.

"This fellow," he said to himself, "is constantly asking that I bestow on him more gold, when I've already given him quite a lot. Most people just ask for a bit of help on New Year's—but this chap is mumbling my name morning, noon and night!"

And the truth was that it had been some time that Eunuch Sung had been without luck. If he ever gambled, he lost. If he made a little investment on the side, it would always turn out bad. And yet, despite all this, every day he grew richer than the day before. But this was not due to luck, but rather to his unethical behavior.

When looking over the books of merchant Wang, he'd put a lapse in his scrutiny if a few ingots of silver found their way into his shirt sleeve. People were always sending him gifts—rolls of silk, fancy foods, etc.—and in return he would turn a blind eye to their misdeeds. But when it came to the poorer folks, it wasn't for any favor that he demanded graft. His gang would extract money from everyone—from butchers and booksellers, restaurateurs and melon girls.

"I deny the mouths of my own children rice, just so Sung can gain more fat around his waist," said Feng Cheng, the seller of pickled shrimp.

"How can I make money when without-a-penis Sung takes all my profit?" said Po Chu, the paper and brush merchant on Brotherly Love Road.

The tax collector loved flowers and dog meat. He liked his flowers in pretty vases and his dog meat cooked with green onions. He was neither a man, nor a woman—but he certainly wasn't starving, had countless costly garments, carpets of ta-deng cloth, slept on a bed of aloes wood, and was feared by many. But who loved him?

Sometimes, when alone, he would cry. He was a dreamer who dreamed and would often ask himself why he had been born—was it for a reason?—feeling somewhat lost in the infinite world.

He sat on a silk cushion in his boudoir, trimming a miniature western palace crab apple in a pretty square pot, delicately cleaning its leaves, while sipping on tea— on fragrant Stone Cliff White from the Neng-jen Temple of Chien-an.

On the wall behind him was a scroll depicting *Cicadas and Butterflies amid Eggplants*, by Diao Guangyin. A painting by Huang Chü-ts'ai, *Hibiscus and Rabbit in Autumn*, hung on the wall before him. On a small wooden table in one corner sat a beautiful rock from Lingbi, which emitted a most enticing aroma. In another corner, an exquisitely carved jade dragon sat on a side table of yellow flowering pear. Objects of beauty and rarity gave comfort to Eunuch Sung, just as the foam of breakers comforts some desolate shore, where nothing grows but sorrows.

"This world of dust, this world of dust . . ." he murmured to himself. "This little western palace crab apple is so much better than I—for what am I but some cherry-apple flower, nice to look at but without fragrance."

Presently, his servant, a little fellow by the name of Tsu Lü, came in and bowed.

"Sir, Purple Bearded Meng-fu is here to see you . . . with a few of the gang."

"Tell them to come back another time. I'm busy."

"Sir, they look quite . . ."

Eunuch Sung grumbled a bit as he rose to his feet. He went out to the courtyard. There they were, all beaten up—their heads bent and bodies drooping like rain-soaked sorghum in autumn.

Sung clicked his tongue and shook his head.

"Sir," Purple Bearded Meng-fu said, "Wild Ch'ing-t'ung and I and these other lads were doing the rounds, but . . ."

He looked at the ground and sniffed.

"Some kid . . ." Wild Ch'ing-t'ung murmured. "Something about a debt . . ."

"A fight . . ."

"A fight?" Eunuch Sung asked. "With who?"

"This kid . . . with tattered sandals."

Later, when Eunuch Sung was back in his boudoir, fingering his cold tea:

"Who would dare beat up my people?" he said to Tsu Lü.

"It sounds like it was some culprit from the lower classes."

"He got the better of Meng-fu!"

"And Meng-fu is so tough!"

"Yes, the bastard must have had training."

"It seems not unlikely, sir."

"Ah, even the beggars are now learning kung fu," Sung lamented. Really, there was very little precious left in the world.

35.

After the incident Pi Wei was a bit worried that the authorities would come and try to grab him, so decided he had better hurry out of town. East Gate was a lot closer than West Gate, so, having grabbed up his sack of millet, he headed in that direction, passing through the execution grounds, by the heads of criminals in cages, going up New Song Road, turning on Horse Street, and then through Better Than Home Lane.

There were good-looking young men—opera singers and actors—hanging about with smiles on their faces, hoping to make some extra cash by getting clients into their kiln. Chaps standing before tea rooms; a fellow asking for a chess partner, another resting on his heels and whispering a poem.

The four categories of people ebbed and flowed, *shi* and *nong, shang* and *gong.* Litterateurs, zither players, damaged acrobats, lusty gamblers, bad monks and good lechers. A young scholar is looking for a back door. A packman has walked all the way from Taiping, and wouldn't mind a spot of fun.

As he passed by the flower houses, Pi Wei admired the women standing in the doorways, cracking melon seeds with their teeth and looking the men up and down. He wondered if holding one of them would be as nice as holding a tree.

"Hey, why don't you come in and let me pour you a few glasses of wine?" one said. "You won't be sorry when you find yourself embracing the dawn with me, I'll bet."

She was about forty *sui* and rather plump.

He laughed and shook his head.

"You think I'm too old for you?"

"No, ma'am. My mistress is much older than you, so that isn't the problem. But how could I dare let you bestow on me your charms, when I have already given my heart to another?"

"Ah, she's a lucky one," the woman murmured.

Pi Wei got to East Gate and went through. The guards didn't even look at him.

"I was overreacting," he thought. "Now I will have to take the long way round to get to Master T'uan's hut."

There were cherry trees in bloom. A wind came along and blew blossoms onto the road before him.

In front of a house, he stopped to admire a peach tree which was winking a thousand ecstatic tones. Casting his glance at the residence itself, he found it to be quite charming. The premises were neat and tidy.

Towards the back of the place there was a kitchen garden in which a woman of a certain age was working, blending manure with the soil. Pi Wei thought of his father—he would bring night soil to women like her, so they could nurture their gardens with it. He took a few steps in her direction; observed and smiled as he watched her do the work, feeling a sense of nostalgia. For a moment he thought he knew her, but then dismissed the thought.

She looked up and saw Pi Wei and nodded her head.

"It's a big garden," he said. "You will have many vegetables this year."

"I hope so," she replied. "But no one can tell the future."

She seemed somewhat nervous. Sadness sat in her eyes. Pi Wei wondered where her family was. Had her children died of smallpox? Had her husband been killed by war?

"What are you going to plant this year?" he asked.

"I normally plant all sorts of things. I love radishes, but for the last two years they've come out somewhat woody—and it's probably too late to plant them anyhow."

Pi Wei nodded his head.

"If you like them, you should try them again. Maybe this year will be different. Maybe it isn't too late."

"Maybe."

Seeing her bent over, distributing the dung over the earth, he had a sudden desire to help her.

"Older Sister," he said, dropping his sack and running up. "Please, allow me."

He grabbed the basket and began to scatter its contents about. Handling the shit filled him with a sense of comfort. The odor was strong and almost brought tears to his eyes.

Some are high
and some are low;
heaven is up
and I am down.

My heart
it floats
just like a cloud
in the sky,
reaches out
like a fern.

Time
it seems yet
just a game.

Crimson petals
they make
me cry
as they fall
around my
memories.

Pi Wei helped her for a while and then she served him
a cup of tea. He looked at her face. It was somewhat tired-
looking, but he imagined she must have, at one time,
been a great beauty. At one time she must have had a face
like a begonia and a body like a poppy. But now—did
she simply sigh like bamboo and wonder about things
that might have been?

As he walked away, he remembered where he had seen her. Her face was very much like Tzu-ku, the goddess who had visited him in his dreams. The thought made him rather melancholy. Even a beautiful woman like that would age—her beauty might fade with time.

On his way back, he plucked an orchid and tucked it behind his ear. He suddenly felt excessively happy—could not wait to get back so he could visit his love. In this season was not her hair, after all, in the latest fashion?

He gathered up a portion of wine from the cave hiding place, but did not go directly to the hut, instead sidestepping that location and proceeding to the forest where he had vigorous sex with Susu.

36.

"Practice the first two, but ignore the third."

"The third?"

"You're no black dragon, so you'd better keep your tail between your legs."

"So the third style . . . ?"

"Just don't do it!"

"But doesn't practice make——"

"No!"

"Master!"

"At the age of nine, it is acceptable for someone to learn the *Classic of Filial Piety*; at the age of twelve, the *Doctrine of the Mean*; at thirty, the inner chapters of the *Tso Wang T'u*; at thirty-five, the *Ssu ling ching*; and at forty, the *Handbook of the Emperors Yao and Shun*. But at what age would it be advisable to learn the inner chapters of the *Mysterious Scripture of Tree Sex Inscribed by the Worthy of the Big Dipper*? Certainly not before a man has reached the age of three or four hundred! As I keep saying—ignore those chapters and stick to the outer chapters . . . or just give the book back to me."

"Don't worry, Master—it is hard enough for me to understand the outer chapters, how could I dare so much as glance at the inner?"

Eye-bright elephant
sparkles like the sunlight,
like a white moonbeam.
The cool spring breeze
is irrevocably pleasant.
The forests they smile;
and clouds breathe the smell of time.

Contrary to Master T'uan's advice Pi Wei began to practice Black Dragon Swinging its Tail. He was, after all, not an inferior fellow—and he found that the practice gave him great delight. He felt power swelling within him. His fingers and toes tingled, his mind felt sharp, his breath flowed freely.

37.

Sayings of Master T'uan:

"The best wine has harmonious energy, but is hard to come by. Forced to drink bad wine, a man's head spins about on his shoulders. But letting go of the head, there is still the heart."

"You can kill someone instantly or deliver a blow that will not kill them for a year."

"One should not put too much trust in rivers, tigers, or men of great wealth."

"It is fine to become a hero. But even among ten thousand heroes, can a single sage be found?"

"Heaven energy promotes earth growth. When heaven energy is lacking, trees die."

"Sometimes I awake feeling queer. The best course of action at such a time is to go back to bed."

"If you know how to breathe, you can live without food for weeks and without water for days."

"I'm not An-ch'i or the Yellow Emperor, but just an old man who likes to drink wine."

"Make sure one foot is placed firmly on the ground before moving with the other. A person should not abandon an old place for a new before testing it well."

"Some people think they can learn just by studying books, but without oral transmission they're like a sword made by a carpenter."

"Why would I need the seven necessities when I can drink the moon from my wine bowl?"

"A pond is extremely sensitive to rain. It begins to quiver, rings forming on its surface, before a man can feel the first drop."

"Wearing rags, I don't have to worry about changes in fashion."

"If your opponent weighs two hundred catties, it just means he will fall down harder."

"Of the nine orifices, only seven can be closed. Regarding the nine pneumas, each must surge and gush without being hampered. If they don't surge and gush without being hampered, how can one attain excellence?"

38.

In the wind, the branches sway back and forth, like a woman agitating a fan.

> Suddenly,
> so suddenly he saw a million flowers open before him;
> and suddenly he perceived so many rays of light;
> so suddenly he could see every speck of dust.
> Suddenly,
> suddenly he could hear everything.

Pi Wei sat, his head leaning against the trunk.

"When I first touched you," he murmured, "it was only desire that I felt—first the desire to improve my fist energy, as Master said I should, and then the desire of actual special contact, as Master warned me of. I thought of you as an object to use—some immobile lady of easy virtue." He let out a sigh. "Now I don't want to see any squirrel come near you and I feel great jealousy when I notice a bird alight on one of your branches—for any nest that is built on you should be mine and it is I alone who should taste your twigs. What need have I of a mortal woman, with her eyes and ears, her nostrils and mouth, when I have you?"

He looked up at the tree and smiled oddly.

"So," he continued, "you will entrust your bark to me—your branches and inflorescences to my hands, my lips, and . . . ?"

Who would have thought the son of a night soil collector could be so romantic!

39.

There is a monkey, but it doesn't have a body, only a head, and sits on a rock. Black and horrified some comedy placed up there to look at the giant grass and brave hares come and snicker near it—morning it is wrapped in mist; at night subtly gleaming in the dark.

There was an old man who wrote poems to the exclusion of all else. He forgot his wife, he forgot his son, he forgot his daughter, he forgot sobriety.

Poems. There are many good ones.

> Indigo crickets;
> lost soldiers;
> the taste of bark.

Myriad manifestations return to their source. Countless objectifications submit to their origin. The wife who never wed gives birth to the son who was never born. Meeting transcendental potential, bring up transcendental matters.

40.

This constant dream. Flower alone. Birds so often make
love amidst my branches, but what love is there for me?
I have been waiting for a mast that has been standing for
such a long time. Does the wait know what I was waiting
for? I am waiting like a mast in the fog. My heart when
it's cold, cold like snow?

> Snow melts away.
> Spring comes for me.
> The bright green sounds.
> No need to hurry.
> Great trees take their time to grow.
> Defects lost in clouds and dust.

He is my first time, what I do not know is when I kiss.
He grasped me and held me. When my hair stood under
the sun, I still felt. Targets cannot rely solely on fostering
water and light.

> The sun it rises
> and birds fly
> from my outspread arms.

At first I was comfortable like clouds, into the stream. Next, it was the most beautiful one. He is a really good horn! It was pure because he was his skin! He will see me! I will mark the young man.

My silence is so full!

My nerves so many, so tactile!

Do you love me too much bark? We are the same as one. The most beautiful tree of the forest, blew me through the wind leaves and my blood is low. This is blue, came and my leaves, fluttering in the wind. Birds, squirrels fly over the sky and ran to my feet. Come on, my love. I, you touch me. Because we are exposed to the sweet dusk together, touch me! I am long for you.

41.

He recalled all the books kept in the latrine of the wine shop and would experiment with Susu, now trying something he had read about in *Amorous Tales of Hangchow*, now imitating one of the illustrations found in *Episodes from Lady Chao's Boudoir*.

He sometimes wished that the tree were more flexible, but then would quickly brush aside the thought, reasoning that, what it lacked in flexibility it more than made up for in docility and, as it said in *Gossip of Wanton Women of Chungking*, there is nothing more satisfactory for a man than to sport with a docile concubine.

After consummation, deep energy surged within him; waves of it rising up from his heels and rolling out through his arms and legs—a ceaseless thing, like the waters of West River. When he leapt in the air, his body rose up two *bu*. When he stomped on the ground, the latter resounded like a drum.

Listen to the language of the songbirds.

Gazing at stars through a mirror, she wished that she could feel the breath of the moon. Cups and saucers dance when a nervous person tries to serve tea and cakes. Su-chiao Immortal went to meet the sunset, but met Cheng Yin along the way. The latter promised transmission after forty years.

Ch'ih Ning was abandoned as a baby and brought up by bandits, who made him drink iron-skin wine every day. Later, while walking on a mountain trail, he saw a white dog and tried to kill it, but was unable to and the dog bit him.

Though he had stolen a huge amount of wine, by fall it began to run low. He started to bring back just a half-bucket, and then a third.

"Hey, why so stingy?" Old man T'uan asked.

"Well, it's becoming rare . . . taxes . . . and things."

Boulders get drunk on waterfalls.

Sought to fulfill his dreams in sewers.

An old man stands motionless. He does not sprint or bow. The answer to the question is silence. People are looking for enlightenment on Lotus Flower Peak. The child eating winter melon isn't worried about tigers or wolves.

Moxibustion. Nine storms in ten days.

42.

He woke up one morning and he was an enemy of red. Blood attacked him, tongues attacked him, cherries attacked him.

He beat blood badly. He boxed with tongues. He kicked cherries, kicked cherries, kicked cherries.

Pink. In his quiver he carries anxious arrows.
Green. Veins of lotus leaf are my simple belief.
Pi Wei. Who shall I beat up next?
Blue. You dirty bastard!
Pi Wei. And to hell with you too! Just because you're always hovering above me, do you think you are without faults? Without the lowly ones, how could you be so high?

And so he hit the sky, broke robins' eggs, struck butterflies.

Tongues. Some feet are not feet, some hands are not hands, some tongues are not tongues. Some names cannot be named and some things are not things but are formless. Fish can't be drowned, ashes can't be burnt. Ghosts don't make noise, and light can't be taught. Without nostrils, you can smell a wooden orchid. Without lips, you can kiss the moon. No shapes are fixed. Is the taste of pure water a triangle or a sphere, circle or hexagon?

Ch'in Kao. Some wish to tame dragons, but don't enter the river. Some enter the river, but are unable to tame dragons. It isn't everyone who can do both!

Realgar. I am very red, like a cockscomb. If you fight me you might win, but then who will scare away the vipers?

Pink. Time can't be caught.

Green. Water can't be climbed.

Tongues. Why bother complaining to the Heavenly Theocrat if things don't go right? If earth is but dirt, then space is but fiction. Ignoring cyclical binaries and not knowing how to prepare the five minerals, what else can one expect but trouble?

Yellow Emperor. The wise study the foolish, to avoid their errors. The foolish, through study, become wise. Others observe the wise in order to become wise. Many people are astute when it comes to minor concerns, but quite stupid in great ones. If a thousand wise men are each only wise in a minor concern, how can they be called wise?

Generalissimo Chiang Tzu-ya. If you want to catch a tiger, you must enter a tiger's den.

43.

Ts'ui Na was a short man with a thin moustache and lank hair. At first he had only been able to converse with small creeks, their rather pointless babble not unlike that of children—vocabulary limited—directionless dialogue. He listened to the dull gurgling and replied, as one might to a baby.

Then medium-sized streams.

He had spent many years developing his technique.

They complained about the kingfishers nesting on their shores, the men sliding along them in their boats— only the sky crying for them when they were sad.

The great rivers, however, were often deep, profound, their talk as difficult to decipher as the work of some ancient philosopher—Kung-sun Lung or Teng Hsi.

He spoke to the Min and she told him of golden sun on skin, her hat of water hyacinths, how she loved to roar after the rain, swirling riders along her banks during times of war, of crinkling and last year's fragrance.

He spoke to the Jiao and she told him of her romance with a red dragon three *li* in length; she told him of her hair, which grew and grew and could never be cut; of dragonflies, sleeping ducks, sweet mist, and the speeding moon.

The longer rivers tended to talk more slowly and Ts'ui Na recalled with a smile on his face the tedious days he had spent listening to the Yellow River, or the six months he had spent along the banks of the Yangtze, in order to hear a rather trivial account of that great river's argument with Ch'ien-t'ang—and how rude that man really and truly was.

It was from the Liao that he learned the most. Each day he went to her, each day persuaded her to open herself up to him—to tell him of her past, to speak to him of her sentiments and impressions, and gradually a unique bond between the two formed.

Later he composed a book, *Stories Water Told Me*

A discerning fellow would say, "If Ts'ui Na could speak with rivers, why could one not speak with other things—with mountains and meadows, rainbows, trees or bushes?"

44.

It was a clear morning, slightly cool, when Pi Wei set off to town. He had told Master T'uan that it was to fetch more wine, and that he was going to Two Wells Village, not Liulin, and the master had given him the floating cash and told him to hurry as there were only about three or four *sheng* left at the hut.

But he had been dreaming of his father; thinking of his father—his feet, one without a sandal. How he had insisted on providing Pi Wei with some sort of education. His smile, with a slight overbite. His dying words . . .

The truth was that the wine Pi Wei had hidden away—the last of it he had brought to Master T'uan just a few days before.

If even mountains and oceans are impermanent, how could a few jars of wine last forever?

The leaves of the maples had already begun to change color. The shadows of the pines seemed rather long, and purple mist rose up out of the forest.

"I'll be back soon," the young man said—to the brooks, the trees, the gorges, the sky.

On the road he passed a dwelling. Out front a man was chopping wood. Pi Wei could hear the sound of the ax even after he had left the man some distance behind.

A maple tree displayed its wounds; yellow leaves were scattered along the road; a jackdaw was pecking around in the weeds; the parasol tree seemed unprepared.

About halfway to town a few clouds began to linger on the horizon. By the time he got to the city gates, the sky had begun to darken. As he passed through, he noticed the two guards were staring up. One of them murmured to the other something about rain and the other nodded his head.

The streets seemed rather more empty than usual. Walking through Red Seconds Alley, he noticed one dog trying to fornicate with another. On West Father and Son Road a man walked past him with rapid steps.

With a little floating cash he bought himself a bun from a bun seller, proceeded on, and ate it while lingering across the street from Eunuch Sung's place. Around the hour of the goat, the gates opened and Eunuch Sung was trotted out on a sedan chair, followed by a few of his toughs—Purple Bearded Meng-fu, Wild Ch'ing-t'ung, and a few others. The eunuch wore an elegant silk jacket with a catfish pattern and had an umbrella on his lap.

Pi Wei followed, and then, when they had reached Miss You Avenue, he ran in front and blocked the way, opening wide his arms.

The people carrying the sedan chair were astonished.

"Hey, move! Get out of the way!" one of them shouted.

"What the hell?"

Eunuch Sung bent forward and glared at Pi Wei with curiosity.

"Who is that?" he asked in a peevish tone.

Purple Bearded Meng-fu, however, recognized Pi Wei.

"Sir," he said to Eunuch Sung, "it's that little rat who caused us so much trouble a while back."

"Trouble?"

"The kid with the debt . . . who bruised us."

"Well, get rid of him quickly or I'll be late for my lunch appointment with Vice Commander Yang."

Purple Bearded Meng-fu, Wild Ch'ing-t'ung, and three other men all surrounded Pi Wei.

The "three other men" were:

1. Wang Pa, nicknamed "Lonely Scorpion." Even rocks and sleeping mutes would have been considered verbose in comparison to him.
2. Ch'iao Li-min. The illegitimate son of Regional Inspector Li Ch'ang-chi. Was cast off as a baby and spent his life with a grudge, which he alleviated to some degree by brawling. No formal training, but had a reputation for eye-popping skills.
3. Yin Kuang. A son-in-law of Kuo-chuan Chen. He went around to various schools but everyone refused to teach him kung fu, due to his bad manners. He finally learned a little from a fellow named Shang Lin.

Wild Ch'ing-t'ung attacked with a roundhouse kick, but Pi Wei easily grabbed his leg and, with his iron grip, pulled him forward, yanking his limb out of joint and making him squeal with pain.

"That powerful little cunt can do shit!" Ch'iao Li-min said.

Meng-fu moved in cautiously, but was, for all that, lying prostrate on the ground in a matter of seconds.

He sighed. His condition didn't surprise him.

Ch'iao Li-min whipped his hands about in the air for a few seconds and then, shifting forward rapidly, attempted an overhand punch. Pi Wei's foot, however, came in contact with his groin and the assailant danced back, grabbing his private area in white-hot agony.

Yin Kuang proceeded with jauntiness, delivering several blows which Pi Wei easily avoided. Pi Wei's arms moved very quickly and the man was leaning against a building, gasping and groaning and gathering his breath and waving his hand in a "no more, please" fashion.

Wang Pa, nicknamed "Lonely Scorpion," was the last of the five assistants. Seeing what had happened to the others, he had no plans to simply rely on his fists and feet. He removed a very short sword from his jacket, unsheathed it, and attacked Pi Wei. The latter stepped aside and then delivered a vicious kick to the back of his assailant's head, which rattled his brain and sent him flying down the street.

Eunuch Sung was rather upset. "Someone must teach that damn cat a lesson," he said.

The four underlings carrying the sedan chair set it down and went to help their brothers. They were all sturdy fellows, each trained in martial arts. They were:

1. Yao Yao. The youngest son of Yao Tao. Had studied Lion's Roar style under a certain Mr. Kan.

2. Shu Lo. Second son of Shu Fu, seller of cakes. He had earned himself the nickname "White Duck" since he was often seen floating naked in the river. Trained in Raw Courage Boxing for a summer under Master Ku. A middle-aged woman and her daughter currently depended on him.

3. Chubby Huo. An orphan. He believed himself to be the reincarnation of Generalissimo Wang Tun. He had studied Autumn Mist Boxing for two months at the Vermilion Sparrow Academy. He was a hard worker, but lacked clearly defined goals.

4. Yao Yu. The younger sister of Yao Yao. She went about disguised as a man, but no one had yet figured this out. She knew a smattering of General Yue Fei's Family Boxing style and was uninhibited in her manners.

45.

Yao Yao. I will kill this waste and may get a raise in salary.

Pi Wei. Your Lion's Roar pattern really makes me laugh. Excuse me while I punch your cheeks.

Yao Yao's Cheeks. Once we belonged to a cute little lad who was happy with fruit and sweets and would stretch us out with his smile, but now we are faced with wretchedness and collapse. It seems the joy was like a bird's nest built in a mortar!

Shu Lo. They call me White Duck, and I can duck and bob. I will tear off this fellow's fingers, and thereby show my courage. How can I cede this road to a lousy moron?

Pi Wei. You have had a lot of sex with the old woman and thus sacrificed your energy. You should have done like me and found a good tree to be your girlfriend. Now I really shall hurt you. How can one who cavorts with unsavory types get the better of me?

Chubby Huo. The time has arrived for me to show my power and the time has arrived for me to show what I can do. In my past life I caused a ruckus and gained great fame, so why in this one should I be known only for holding up a single corner of the tax collector's sedan chair?

Pi Wei. Glutted on starches and high-in-fat foods, can you contend with me? You should really just rest under the restroom like other pigs I've known.

Yao Yu. My older brother by you was defeated, but this does not mean a damn thing. Shu Lo and Chubby Huo were weak compared to me. Men think they rule the world, and in doing so treat jade like grass and silk like dirt. Could the lowing of cattle ever be compared in beauty and elegance to the song of the whistling thrush?

Pi Wei. You look like a man, but I have my suspicions.

Yao Yu. Watch my foot as it flies at your face. Look at my hands as they weave towards your chest.

Pi Wei. Yes, you've got in a few strikes, but now it's time for me to let you feel your inadequacy. You really need to find a better boss! With so much laxity you're bound to get hurt!

46.

Eunuch Sung's people were all lying in the lane, in great discomfort, unable to fight further.

"It looks like I'll have to take care of this rascal myself," the eunuch said.

He was forced to rise from his seat. The whole incident had put him in a bad mood. It was likely he would be late for his luncheon engagement, and the idea annoyed him greatly. A frown pulled at his plump cheeks.

"Who the hell are you?"

"You bastard, I guess you don't remember the son of the man you killed."

"I suppose not," he said. "If I can't remember the father, how could I remember the son?"

"My father was Pi Jung, and I'm his son Wei. My father was a lowly night soil carrier, but his spirit cannot rest easy until I crack your head into several pieces."

Eunuch Sung laughed. "A little workout before lunch," he murmured. "I'll eat well after I break all this bamboo rat's bones."

Stupid lad,
move yourself from my path;
tiny frog,
I too can hear you laugh.

"I want to test your dirty fist!" Pi Wei said.

"I want to punch your puny face!"

"I want to rip up your foul smile!"

Pi Wei attacked. Eunuch Sung, after warding off a few blows, realized that he didn't have a normal fellow to deal with. Pi Wei showed himself to be both supple and strong. He moved with confidence, was not shy in his offensives. Clearly he had been studying under some formidable teacher.

Eunuch Sung began to turn to the right, as if he wished to walk away, but when Pi Wei moved in on him, he spun to the left, delivering a haymaker punch into the young man's chest, sending pain surging through him.

Pi Wei coughed and wobbled his head.

"That's the fist that killed my father!" he thought, and was filled with anger. He bent his body in Taoist enlightenment posture and regained his composure; then shot a swinging kick towards Eunuch Sung's midsection, but the latter moved aside with ease and delivered a leopard's paw strike. Pi Wei bobbed his head out of the way, but heard a whooshing sound as the eunuch's hand moved by his ear. Pi Wei Launched a tiger tail kick, but this was parried by Sung.

The echoes of their blows could be heard up and down the street.

Eunuch Sung twirled about, as if he were a maiden spreading flowers in the air. Pi Wei blocked high and low, as if he were a devotee picking fruit and laying it at an altar. A few people who had been wandering down the road stopped and looked on. One man at first mistook it for a street performance.

"How elegant!"

"That fat fellow is as lithe as a child!"

"Oh! But the young man . . . he's quite something!"

Pi Wei was like a happy lad playing in a field. He spun around like a plate on a stick. His fists cut through space; he was like a demon scattering chaos over the earth. No one would have been surprised if he had blown black smoke out of his nostrils or spat rods of lightning from his mouth. He stalked about like a panther and then leapt like a tiger; gored like a bull and bucked like a horse; hurled blows as if they were stones and delivered kicks as if he were trying to batter down castle walls.

Eunuch Sung was as fat as a furry rabbit, but quite agile—a hungry hawk looking to get blood on its wings. His body whirled this way and that. He performed a dazzling series of moves that few could follow. His feet were as small as a nine-year-old girl's and his footwork was now like silkworms on mulberry stems, now like crabs scurrying on sand. He seemed like Hsi Wang Mu dancing on clouds. His arms cut through the air, reaching and reaching.

Pi Wei found himself in one of the eunuch's locks— he agitated his feet, tripped Sung up, and freed himself. The eunuch then attacked with a crane's beak strike, but Pi Wei swiveled to the right avoiding the blow and then returned the favor with a strike known as "eye of the phoenix," which landed on Sung's shoulder, causing him some agitation.

Eunuch Sung nodded his head.

"This little bitch hasn't been idle," he said aloud.

"I am honored that my humble skills excite you!"

Eunuch Sung used strike upon strike, but Pi Wei's blocks stuck to them like rice to a serving spoon. Pi Wei lunged with a tiger's claw, but Sung parried with a white crane wing. Pi Wei launched a middle reverse round-house kick at the eunuch's stomach; the latter was unable to parry it and tumbled backward.

"You scum," he said with annoyance.

The eunuch landed a butterfly kick on Pi Wei's shoulder.

"Dog without a tail!" Pi Wei said.

A strong wind rolled through the town, stirring up dust. A few drops of water fell on the dry earth, sending off a pleasant aroma.

Ch'ih Sung-tzu. I came from the K'un-lun Mountains just to watch this dispute.

Mysterious Disembodied Voice. Is that Liang Fu down there?

Ts'ai Tan. No, just the son of a shit carrier.

Mysterious Disembodied Voice. Still, he seems sincere.

Ts'ai Tan. And I was too. I read all the classics, but where did that get me?

Huai Hui. Concentrate on the essential; ignore the vagaries.

Ch'ih Sung-tzu. They're having quite a battle!

Ts'ai Tan. Fighters fight. It's what they do.

Nāgārjuna. How can the agent and action be identical?

Dharmapāla. Yes, otherwise how could we distinguish Pi Wei from his fists?

Chandrakīrti. Or Eunuch Sung from his feet.

Hui Chung. Some people never speak; some over-speak. Innumerable performance return to their origins; innumerable objectifications obey their source. Essence and motion: a bitter experience, a response. Perforation and penetration: one thrust, one parry. Hold and releases: an entrance, an exit.

[When Hui Chung was sixteen, while sweeping the porch according to mother's instructions, he heard a clergy reciting the religious text which says: "Thought is not the composition of form, does not make concrete, cannot radiate, cannot touch, not exterior or among lives in its interior. The mind has not extricated, because its instinct is the comprehensive reality." Hearing these words, he had an experience, abandoned the broom, ran across the bridge, directly soared to the Buddhist priest, bowed low and deep. "Good afternoon. Where do you come from?" "As if attempt on the cow following snow and hoof add the frost. You increase the mistake wrongly, and rub the brick to make the mirror. You are dragging through the mud in Pingjiang."]

<h1 style="text-align:center">47.</h1>

The onlookers, gazing up at the sky, sticking out their hands and feeling the drops land on them, for the most part decided it was time to depart—they didn't wish to get wet. And as interesting as it was to watch these two fellows twirl around in the street and slap each other, one couldn't just stand there staring all day—for street performances usually didn't last so long!

After about twenty bouts, neither Pi Wei nor Eunuch Sung seemed to have achieved a clear advantage. Getting revenge was tougher than Pi Wei had expected. He wondered how that old eunuch could be so formidable.

The truth was, however, that Eunuch Sung was beginning to feel rather winded. He hadn't been training much and, as of late, had been spending a lot more time drinking wine and eating meat than stretching his limbs and doing his drills. Still, he figured given the right opening he would get the better of this young punk who seemed so set on ruining his day. Right about then Vice Commander Yang would be wondering where he was. The wine was probably already on the table with some preliminary snacks.

The eunuch made play, advancing and thrusting, pressing and plunging. Wei dodged and blocked, evaded and parried. Sung splashed with a long series of kicks. The young man blocked them with his legs and counter kicks. So a short melee ensued, legs to legs. Pi Wei kicked Sung in the groin, but it did not have its desired effect. The son of Jung delivered a hook punch to the eunuch's face, but the latter ducked and landed a palm on the ribs of the former.

> Whores they smile,
> maggots crawl without love;
> sleeping grain,
> clouds are breathing above.

They exchanged blows at close quarters, but Sung was tired, and his fists seemed ineffectual, while Pi Wei seemed as if he were vigorously pounding a drum. He let off barrage after barrage of strikes. The eunuch blocked what he could, but for every one that he blocked two found their mark. Pi Wei connected with a shark tooth strike to the chest, and Eunuch Sung was stunned.

Water was falling from the sky, going pitter-pat on the earth.

Eunuch Sung was swaying on his legs. He seemed to be having difficulty standing.

Pi Wei punched him in the face, then moved in behind him and performed a strike called "removing the general's helmet." Eunuch Sung grimaced horribly; his eyes rolled back in his head and blood began to gush from his mouth; when Pi Wei released him, he fell to the ground. The eunuch's eyes were wide open, but he was no more alive than a stone or a doorframe.

The rain was coming down swiftly now, bringing joy to trees and foliage and in the countryside the rivers and marshes were drinking their fill, and the last pears were weighed down by this welcome guest.

Blood was flowing freely from Eunuch Sung's nose and mouth, red turning to pink as it mixed with the water from the sky. His eyes were open and his silk jacket was dirty. His arm was twisted in an odd position.

The sedan chair was off to one side, water beading up on its polished seat, Sung's umbrella sitting there useless, a forgotten thing. Where were Sung's men? They were nowhere around. Wild Ch'ing-t'ung would take up the job as assistant-manager-in-training of the Perpetual Harmony Inn in Two Wells Village his uncle had been offering him for some time. Purple Bearded Meng-fu would hire himself out as a rough to trade groups making illegal transactions—but his stock had fallen. Wang Pa, nicknamed "Lonely Scorpion" falls in love with Chuang Jing and begins to write poetry. Ch'iao Li-min becomes homeless. Yin Kuang is told by his wife that it is time he "get a real job." Yao Yao and Shu Lo go into the salted seafood business together. Chubby Huo joins White Stream Monastery as a novice. Yao Yu gets married to a fellow named Liu Chung-fu, has many children who she tells stories about scholarly lizards, magic lotuses, and her exciting youth.

Pi Wei's heart should have been filled with glee, but it wasn't. He felt tired, listless. Was his father's spirit happy now?

He turned and started to walk away.

It was at this point that a group of soldiers came up—not exactly at a run, but they were walking fast.

"STOP STOP STOP!" they cried out.

They arrested Pi Wei. He could have resisted, but he felt downhearted and limp. The soldiers led him off through the muddy streets, their feet splashing aggressively in puddles.

That night he slept in jail, on some dirty hay.

48.

Master T'uan poured the last of the wine into his cup. Pi Wei had disappeared several days before, not long after having given the teacher that last jar.

"That youngling," he murmured, "he left me here to wither away in thirst. In the past, when I was addicted to starches and meat, a half a jar of wine would get me quite drunk. Now, however, that I only snack on herbs, nibble a few pine needles, etc. it takes a good deal to let me arrive at intoxication. In the third month, when the sorghum wine is ready, I can drink an entire *hu* and not even feel the effects. I drink thick country wine and it feels as if I had just wet my lips. New wine is green in color and suits me just fine. Drinking celestial yellow dew, would I even become tipsy? Poor Ku Yüeh—his hair turned white before its time all due to his having taken up the burden of government affairs. To the just hatched chick, every sound seems like the sound of thunder. The tortoise moves slowly, but lives for countless years. At the market, the ladder-seller stands proud, but his wares can hardly let one ascend to the clouds. Some act like they are immortal at the age of fifty, claiming that they know

Heaven's Decree, yet their sperm is dead and their ears plugged with yellow wax. Some brag about their thousand-*li* legs, but find themselves short of breath after one hundred steps. Pines they sway in the wind. Mushrooms grope beneath the ground. The best wine gets you drunk, without ever tasting strong. The great general defends, but never attacks. The bonds of society? What comfort are they to a man when his bones become ashes? If one loses one's primordial nature, where shall one look to find it? Does one ever catch a whale by casting a line into the shallows of a pond? Shallows and deeps; when the moon is at its nadir, the sun is at its zenith. Striving after what is not needed, what is needed is ignored. Ta-chi was a woman of great beauty, yet caused the downfall of Shang. Chung-li Chün was a woman of unparalleled ugliness, but saved the state of Ch'i. Men with leisure discuss the merits of this or that system of thought while still being ignorant of how to walk on water or create amulets for charming mountains. Some build themselves grand houses and settle down to work in the Six Ministries, thinking thereby that they have become stable. Worms burrow into the earth and birds float about in the sky. The sage, however, realizes that everything fluctuates— the sky churns, the earth rumbles—and so he is always prepared to step forward or retreat, as the situation requires. Striding through mountains, dancing over brooks. Drinking the Yangtze at a draught, consuming Mt. T'ai with a swallow. Thunder can roar above heaven; mountains can sit beneath earth. Thunder above heaven is mature. A mountain sitting beneath earth is humble. The most profound scriptures are written on the fluttering leaves of a tree. Listen closely and hear the wind preach on the essential truths of the Way. Discerning right and wrong—isn't it a matter of perspective? In this world of causal origination, some go about with their mouths open, some with their mouths shut. Open, he goes astray; shut, he is unable to advance. Some are eager to accept burdens, but cast them aside midway. Others are chary to take on new duties, but once taken on, will perform them with the utmost diligence. Sun Ch'o planted a pine tree in front of his residence, thinking he would grow old with her, but he only lived to be thirty-five—surely because he went too far!"

49.

Sorrows float like mist. The moon, like a fingernail, scratches gently at the night. The meaning of the ancient implements has been forgotten. Weeds grow high around the remnants of long-past luxury.

In Burma, there is a kind of jade known as "moss entangled in melting snow." Even purity is tricky. Monasteries and convents are, after all, full of books.

If Master Useless got busy, he could change the age. When high positions are tossed away, like rotten fruit, the snow clears on the mountain peaks. The white pine seed already contains a thousand-*chang* tree, with knots and fungus, beauty and shade. An effect must have a cause; a cause must have an effect. Has one ever seen a goer who doesn't go, or going without a goer?

Under the ancient trees
I stretch my limbs,
living in great simplicity.
So keep your city,
I'll take my way,
travelling among
mountains and streams.

Some read a hundred sutras, and don't recall a line. Some
read the entire Seventeen Dynastic Histories, but don't
learn a thing. Who ever heard of feathers sinking or
stones floating?

The eccentric sexual habits of the adept.

A juniper tree,
a primitive emerald,
fleeting daytime dream.

Hillside juniper;
a throne of elegant rocks

reached by distant sounds;
chatter of water and birds;
on this star, another day.

Smell of juniper,
some celestial perfume;
touching its soft bark;
serried hills of soft skin.

50.

Eunuch Sung's mother was eighty *sui*. When she heard what had happened to her son, she wept profusely.

"Ah, what a bad mother I've been," she thought. "I let my son become a gelded steed—a fellow for the nobility to ride about without him causing them problems. Now, in generations to come, who will offer wine to his ghost? What a great sin you've committed, my son, dying before your mother! You really always were such a naughty boy! . . . I remember when you were born, how painful it was—how I screamed and cried! . . . And growing up you caused me so much trouble. You would never listen to me. If I told you to go east, you would go west; if I told you to bow, you would leap into the air. I put meat on your rice with my own chopsticks and wiped you with my own hand, treating your body as if it were my own."

> The grass it blows
> in this lonesome wind;
> even the rocks
> are not
> as ugly as I.

The poison pig
snorts its snout
and the crazy toad
it croaks,
as foolish moths
beat against
the window paper.

Occupied night;
dawn eternally incompatible.

But if there were no night
dawn would never come.

Eunuch Sung had provided quite well for her; when
he had moved from the capitol to Liulin, he had brought
her along. He had always given her gifts, bowed to her,
massaged her shoulders, had the chef make her special
cakes, poured her wine on New Year, listened attentively
as she talked about the neighbors, slept next to her when
he was feeling down, complimented her on her figure,
taken her on picnic lunches, helped her adjust her hairpins, made sure the best pears were set aside for her—in
short, he had been a filial son.

51.

Pi Wei's rags were taken away and he was given a coat and trousers of rough red cloth. On the back of the coat, in large characters, was written:

LIULIN PRISON

In his jail cell he sat on his straw, with a cangue around his neck, and felt sad. He thought of the outer world—of Master T'uan's mountain hut and the forest that lay beyond. . . . The thick shade, the birdsong, the smell of pine. . . . And then, of his beloved.

"If only the wind could blow a leaf of my love onto my lap," he thought.

The other prisoners knew that he was in there for murdering an official, and left him alone. They suspected that he wasn't quite mentally stable. Sometimes he would smile or laugh without reason. At others tears would roll down his cheeks. He cast longing glances at nothing and scowled at shadows.

After about a week, Pi Wei, bound in red rope, was brought before the judge. Kneeling, he stated the circumstances of his case—how his father, a humble night soil man, had been unjustly killed by Eunuch Sung—how this had happened and the eunuch had received no punishment whatsoever. His voice quivered with emotion as he told his tale.

The judge was a short man, with large eyes and somewhat sympathetic features. As Pi Wei spoke, he nodded his head.

"I should just sentence this lad to a good flogging and be done with it," he thought. "He was, after all, simply performing his filial duty. One cannot very well share the land under heaven with the murderer of one's father. As it says in Ch'in Li's *Subcommentary on the Meaning of the Kung-yang Commentary* (In the *Ch'un ch'iu chuan*), 'A son who does not avenge his father is not a good son.' And the one who got killed was nothing more than a eunuch—someone incapable of helping our country along at all. He had a reputation for hassling people, accepting bribes, and absconding with taxes meant for the state. Ah, these damned eunuchs—the royal family would do well to not allow them to be sniffing around the Royal Palace and slipping their paws into the state coffers. Indeed, how many people around town must have wished Eunuch Sung dead? Surely I can go soft on the one who dealt with him."

Just as the judge was reasoning in this manner, however, a lady came striding in—her features sharp, her face a frown. One of the guards raised an eyebrow and smirked. She squinted her eyes, piercing Pi Wei with her gaze.

"You finally caught him!"

"And who are you?"

"I'm this rascal's ex-employer. My name is Mrs. Wang. My husband and I own the Good Time Wine shop on Hundred Chang Alley."

"Ah, the place that used to have the famous clean latrine!"

"That's right. This fellow you have before you, this Pi Wei, is the one we used to employ to keep it clean. So it isn't that he is absolutely without virtue. But then he went lax and began to neglect his duties. He started robbing from us—slipping us tricky cash and robbing us of our best wine—pecule upon pecule! He disappeared and our latrine became extremely untidy and the number of clients and money we lost is countless and so we had to fire him. When I heard that he had been arrested for killing Tax Collector Sung, I thought I had better get over here and set things straight about his character."

"Hmm," the judge said, nodding his head, "it seems this fellow has a history of misbehavior. I was going to be lenient with him since he struck me as a pitiful character, but instead I think it would be best if, after a proper flogging, he had his nose chopped off."

"NO!"

The voice was loud and mean and everyone was surprised to hear it.

"No?"

"NO!"

Now another person pushed themselves forward. It was an old lady, leaning on a bamboo staff, unable to bear her years or hardships, and wearing a costume of unhemmed sackcloth—the clothing of mourning. Her face was a maze of wrinkles and tears. She was as shaky as an aspen leaf in the fall. Looking at her, everyone was filled with unease.

"No, no, no—this cannot be, judge!" she said in her quaking voice. "How can you think of letting this rascal go with everything but his nose? How can you think of such a thing, when he has murdered my son—my precious Chü-i? Yes, my son, a court eunuch—a Royal Tax Collector—a representative of the Emperor himself. This young man, this low fellow, murdered his superior—so how can that not be even worse than if he had murdered his own father? He murdered the servant of the Emperor—how horrible is that? Is it not true, after all, that of the five social relationships, that which exists between sovereign and subject is the most precious?"

"That could be true, but . . ."

Old Lady Sung, however, was not interested in hearing any "buts." She was a real rhetorician—one who would have made the mothers of Chiang Chu or Pi-hsi jealous with her ability.

"Were not laws made to restrain the defiant ones?" she said. "If the crime is heavy and the punishment is light, then the wicked will feel no need to control themselves. Not controlling themselves, they show contempt for the Son of Heaven. If this were to happen, then how could disaster be avoided? How could killing a government official not be considered an act of great irreverence—one of the ten abominations? You speak of going soft on his offense by merely having him beaten and cutting off his nose, but on what grounds can you do such a thing, since he is neither a child, an old man, or one disabled? On the contrary, he is a young man in the full vigor of life, who clearly has his wits about him. Why hesitate? On his seventh day in office, Confucius had Shao-cheng Mao executed. Duke Wen of Chin had Chieh's head removed from his shoulders. Hua Yüan executed T'ang Shan. King Chuang saw that Hsia Cheng-shu was put to death. Duke Chi, knowing his duty, executed his own brothers. Emperor Wu, showing leadership ability, administered the death penalty to his nephews. When something is no good, one has to get rid of it. Even the best cook can't make a tasty dish from badly rancid meat."

The judge had issued many punishments in his time. He had ordered to have countless people castrated and three times as many branded. He had had people's knee-caps cut off, and their eyebrows cut away and the tendons of their necks clipped—had had people cut into twenty-four pieces, or sometimes thirty-six pieces, or sometimes seventy-two pieces, or sometimes one hundred and twenty pieces. He didn't mind delivering harsh sentences. It was, after all, his job. He didn't care much for this old lady or the fate of her castrated son—but it was clear that she was one of those noisy types who wouldn't let the matter drop. As the old saying goes, "In the end, the pushy ones always get their way."

He scratched his chin and then, after letting out a little sigh, delivered the sentence:

"The criminal will be executed."

52.

The executioner was a bald old man with dark, clever-looking eyes. He was not very tall, but carried a huge, double-edged sword—an item that seemed to be almost as large as he was. He was bare-footed and wore loose, rather dirty clothing. Indeed he looked like one of those lower-end butchers at the market who would sell dubious meats—old chickens and brown, fly-covered slabs of "beef."

There were three executions he had to do that morning—the fellow who had killed Eunuch Sung, another fellow by the name of Tun-kuo Yen, whose crime was "being troublesome," and a nameless mute, who had been convicted of burglary.

The victims were all carried out in baskets and deposited in the execution grounds at the east end of the market place, where a small crowd had gathered to watch the proceedings, to be filled with the thrills of both horror and delight—for, seeing horrible things inevitably brought strong feelings to some.

There were three sedge mats laid out, one for each criminal.

Pi Wei climbed out of his basket. His hair hung down unbound, unkempt, giving him a wild look. He was told to kneel. For a moment he thought of resisting, of trying to fight his way out of the situation—but it was only for a moment, an instant. Had not the judge condemned him to die? Did he, Pi Wei, son of Pi Jung, wish to become a rebel and disgrace his father's name? He had had his revenge, so how could he complain of the results? Laws were, after all, laws.

The executioner danced around for a few moments and then, stopping and raising his sword high, pressed his lips tightly together. The blade swung down and Pi Wei's neck left his body—and then the old man moved on to the other executions he had to do that morning— *can't be clumsy one stroke and it's done a heavy blade see their eyelids bat see their eyelids close necks blood-clad fallen flower in this autumn wind* and later he would see their faces reflected in his wine, can you smell it the blood that's been shed today?

The Executioner's Crippled Wife. How is it that you always manage to cut them off with a single stroke?
The Executioner. Practice makes perfect!
Liang K'ai. That's what I keep saying.
The Snowgoose. I have no desire to fly lower.
Ch'i and Lin. We have no wish to gallop slower.
Ta Hui. The best thing is not to stop halfway. If Ch'i and Lin were half as fast, who would speak of their speed? If the snowgoose flew half as high, who would comment on how high it flies? Do you think sitting cross-legged for twenty-five days is enough?

Pi Wei's head was put in a cage, which was then elevated onto a pole for display, with the heads of other criminals, right there in the east end of the market—so people could see what happened to bad fellows.

53.

A Taoist walks through the mountains—past grand rivers and through bamboo forests that shine greenly.

"Unsullied wisdom, it has no right or wrong," he chants, in a cavernous, expressive and doleful voice. "If a man wishes to become a sage, he must abandon obligations, abandon duties. Go slowly. Be observant. If no one understands you, how can you be called a genius? The iris is my bed, the Fu star my roof. Pine needles are my feast, red panicled-millet wine my drink. When people see me, they mistake me for withered grass. A firefly hangs from each strand of my hair. Delightful, dimensional, marvelous and ineffable. The tiger fingernail, the dog blood. Old rocks are my friends, so I'm never alone. Owl's never fly in groups. Don't mess with mountains or you mess with mountain gods. On good days the Travelling Canteen appears before my eyes. I nibble on sweet mushrooms and snack on bright mica, intoning immortality's tune. I eat geodes with wild honey, and get high on sky sperm. In spring, I am green; in autumn, red—this is because I am jade. When you drink wine you should use blue cups with brown rims. The inside should be painted with reeds. The cups should be deep and filled to overflowing to cause drunkenness. Kao Lin drank fourteen cups of wine while sitting in the sun. He sweated a great deal. Can your body? If you have high pictorial skill, that is best. Next best is to have no pictorial skill. Paint on the wood a figure with six arms, at least one of which holds an etiquette dagger. He stops danger using bundles of golden leaves. Melts tigers. Blocks ghosts who swallow swallow."

Acting on impulse, General Yang ate Section Subordinate Wu's eyeballs, but they got stuck in his throat.

Mi Yung got married twice on the same day. King Wen subsisted on pickled vegetables. Chewing on poetry, one finds it bitter. Drinking proper diction, one finds it bland. Wang Hsiang's unkind stepmother would, during storms, have him embrace her favorite crab apple tree to protect it, little knowing that love would eventually blossom.

Chou Fang sounds the jade chimes, hoping thereby to cause rain. P'ing-yi dances, but has no wish to fight with the Earl of the Wind. Chang K'ai ate too many tortoise brains and couldn't sleep for one hundred years.

The wind, blowing through the tree tops, sounded like the ocean.

Kuan Chung cheated Pao Shu, his business partner, and the latter, knowing the former had a mother to support, didn't mind. T'ien Chi collected bribes in order to support his mother, but she declared him an unfilial son. Everything becomes a style if repeated often enough.

A dish of fried cinnabar and varnish honey will make you lose your shadow.

Old man Ch'in touches a withered tree and it bursts into flower. In the morning of deep winter, the sun is hoisted up by some hard-working clouds. A white crown pierced by pines—huge breasts, the milk has frozen over them. In autumn, the breeze, wandering through the mulberry trees, plays an ancient melody.

Once it was very dry. No water for months. The plants were unhappy. The needles of the pines turned brown. Crow called out to the changes, asking for rain. Soon, the rivers were overflowing. Soon, the rivers were turned upside-down.

The money was spent on wine. Thirty thousand cups, or fifty thousand cups. Drunk, go and mate with trees. As you go, they seem to talk, telling tales of curious things. The reason they can talk is because they have a power called *yün-yang*. One needn't have three ears, like Chang Shentong, to hear them, just a little patience and the amorous nature of Jung-ch'eng.

Shun had double pupils and ears with three orifices. Yao had rainbow-colored eyebrows. Liu An could turn himself into a woman at will. Tso Tz'u could make himself appear in twenty-four places at once. Mind is an undetectable percipient, by way of cognition that cannot be explained. Each thought and image of presenting are without witness.

SHOUT!
SHOUT!
SHOUT!

Strips of sunlight,
shit,
hair,
the short side of love,
a lice-covered couple
huddled up,
enjoying their carnal embrace,
drifting to some orchid-scented location,
the sound of insects.

Duke Ching of Ch'i felt little passion for women, instead finding in a parasol tree all that he could wish for. He had a signpost placed before the tree, stating that no one should touch it, and anyone who violated the tree would be executed.

If you have a cloud over your head, better let it go.

54.

MONSTERS HIDE BEHIND ROCKS AND SLINK THROUGH THE UNDERGROWTH, WISHING TO CRACK YOU IN TWO. AVOID GREAT ACTIONS ON TABOO DAYS OR YOU WILL BE EATEN BY WOLVES. SOME SEEM LIKE FRIENDS, BUT WHEN YOU STAB THEM, THEY TURN INTO DOGS.

Pi Wei's head sat in its cage overlooking those who came and went from the market. The children stared up at in horror, shivering.

Normally the heads were left there for some time, until they began to rot and ooze and look exceptionally ghoulish, but after a few days Pi Wei's disappeared.

An old man carries a bundle wrapped in a rag. He carries it into the forest, and, unwrapping it, buries its contents at the base of a tree.

Their only epithalamium is the sighs of the wind.

A discerning fellow would say, "Eunuch Sung overreached and ended up having to justify his behavior before King Ch'in Kuang."

Master T'uan was no longer seen in the area. Only the sky had seen him depart. Seasons came and went. The roof of his hut caved in. In the summer, leaves blew through the dwelling and in the fall rain bathed the floor. Who remembered Master T'uan? Only the beetles and water lilies. Who remembered Master T'uan's disciple?

55.

This constant dream. Whispering alone.

> At dawn, birds fly from their nests.
> At dusk, crows fold in their wings.
> The moon and me,
> we're both
> just ghosts
> waiting for our time.

Standing for so long, like a mast, waiting. Waiting without knowing of love or deep pleasure, my roots sucking up spring water, my leaves drinking in autumn dew. Waiting for summer, waiting for winter, waiting like a mast in the mist. A deer comes and shakes its tail at my trunk. Go away you beastly thing! My heart was spacious and empty. Was it empty and expecting? Was my heart so cold, so cold as drifting snow? Then you came, wishing in some strange way to grapple with me. Did you think you could find love among indifferent trees?

When he kissed me for the first time, I did not know what that was. He grabbed me and held me. And then he sipped from my twig-tips. When I stood under the foot of the sun, I quietly felt. But one cannot be nurtured by water and sun alone. Can the night be indifferent to the moon which floats across its sky? And he was like a cloud, come to water me. At first it was uncomfortable. Then it was the most beautiful thing. Really a good young man! His skin was so pure! He let me own! Were we then deviants? If we were, then it was because we wanted to be different. Playing with you, young man. Did he love my bark so much? We were one. My forty thousand leaves, each one you kissed.

> Things have changed.
> A cricket chirps;
> the night sky
> is high as a hill.

When the east wind blew me through, I sang low, and the sky sang back to me. It was a blue wind that came and fluttered my leaves. And then one day a most beautiful thing happened when you shared your nectar with me and it felt as if heaven and earth had finally become one. Then he lay on the mossy ground at my feet, expelling his sweet sighs. The bird flew over the squirrel and came to my feet. You came on, because I wanted you to tie us together, to touch touch touch me.

Touch me as we touch the sunset together! I yearn for you. How I wish I could have stopped those months we spent together, and turned them into never-ending years. We were together so often, eating the flowers of dawn, him waging on me his constant love. But now I can no longer hear the drumbeat of your heart near me. And now, as I stand here beneath the Milky Way, lost in grief, your head lies buried at my feet. My poor young lover! Oh, how I wish to taste again your purple tongue! The seasons pile one atop the next. Your head now lies buried at my feet, in this constant dream.

56.

Su-nu played her fifty-stringed zither and the Yellow Emperor was moved to tears. Su-nu sang of rivers and lakes and Nu Chi became immortal.

Method for making children never grow up: Take a tortoise egg and place it under a chicken until it hatches; chop the small tortoise up finely and cook it with millet and willow catkins. Feed it to a child you want to never grow up.

A discerning fellow would say, "The Spirit of the Vale should be preserved. Because it was not preserved, disaster followed. The toothless one doesn't nibble on dried deer meat. Inner purity is something many talk about, but who can dare say they possess?"

He noticed that his four limbs had filled the hole. Step on his body. He was ripped to fragments by the wild horse, was bitten by the crazy monkey. Dawn from opening wide in the silver screen to gush out. A middle-aged man wearing a dignified fibroin gown is pulling at a long narrow tube, sitting cross-legged and his eye is touching a small beard.

He will forget to return on the road, practice time in the forest.

Good to laugh.
Smile together.

Nipped thing,
ear,
throat,
lip,
boiled poultry,
thigh,
breast.

Some drinking companions grow mellow and speak of books and worlds made of mysterium, while the mouths of others are stained with plum sauce by the hour of the rooster and by the hour of the pig their fists are swirling through the air. Drinking companions, under a willow, lean against each other, sipping on thick raw wine from the mountain villages and talking cocoons and candles which float into the night. Now, wake up, one arm covered in vomit, the other in the stream.

Rain.
The grass grows endlessly.

A PARTIAL LIST OF SNUGGLY BOOKS

LÉON BLOY *The Tarantulas' Parlor and Other Unkind Tales*

S. HENRY BERTHOUD *Misanthropic Tales*

FÉLICIEN CHAMPSAUR *The Latin Orgy*

FÉLICIEN CHAMPSAUR *The Emerald Princess and Other Decadent Fantasies*

BRENDAN CONNELL *Metrophilias*

QUENTIN S. CRISP *Blue on Blue*

LADY DILKE *The Outcast Spirit and Other Stories*

BERIT ELLINGSEN *Vessel and Solsvart*

EDMOND AND JULES DE GONCOURT *Manette Salomon*

RHYS HUGHES *Cloud Farming in Wales*

JUSTIN ISIS *Divorce Procedures for the Hairdressers of a Metallic and Inconstant Goddess*

VICTOR JOLY *The Unknown Collaborator and Other Legendary Tales*

BERNARD LAZARE *The Mirror of Legends*

JEAN LORRAIN *Masks in the Tapestry*

JEAN LORRAIN *Nightmares of an Ether-Drinker*

JEAN LORRAIN *The Soul-Drinker and Other Decadent Fantasies*

ARTHUR MACHEN *Ornaments in Jade*

CAMILLE MAUCLAIR *The Frail Soul and Other Stories*

CATULLE MENDÈS *Bluebirds*

LUIS DE MIRANDA *Who Killed the Poet?*

OCTAVE MIRBEAU *The Death of Balzac*

CHARLES MORICE *Babels, Balloons and Innocent Eyes*

DAMIAN MURPHY *Daughters of Apostasy*

KRISTINE ONG MUSLIM *Butterfly Dream*

YARROW PAISLEY *Mendicant City*

URSULA PFLUG *Down From*

JEAN RICHEPIN *The Bull-Man and the Grasshopper*

DAVID RIX *A Suite in Four Windows*

FREDERICK ROLFE *An Ossuary of the North Lagoon and Other Stories*

JASON ROLFE *An Archive of Human Nonsense*

BRIAN STABLEFORD *Spirits of the Vasty Deep*

BRIAN STABLEFORD (editor) *Decadence and Symbolism: A Showcase Anthology*

JANE DE LA VAUDÈRE *The Demi-Sexes and The Androgynes*

JANE DE LA VAUDÈRE *The Double Star and Other Occult Fantasies*

RENÉE VIVIEN *Lilith's Legacy*